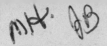

The sunshine streaming in through his uncovered windows made the highlights in her shiny hair glow, and he itched to run his fingers through all those dark and reddish strands.

He tried to think of a word to describe it and couldn't. *Brown* was too plain a term to describe all that lustrous silk.

"What color is your hair?" Oh man, had he actually asked that out loud? What was wrong with him?

"What?" She gave him a quizzical look.

Liam shrugged and hoped his face wasn't as flushed as it felt. "Meg has a thing about people calling her hair red and I, uh, just wondered if you had a name for your color like she does."

She ran a hand over her hair. "It's chestnut. Why?"

Liam nodded, but didn't answer her question. He'd embarrassed himself enough for one day. "Are you planning on telling me why you're here?"

She rubbed her hands on her thighs and drew in a deep breath. "I know we decided this summer was no strings attached, but—"

"About that, Ellie, I—"

"I'm pregnant."

* * *

SMALL-TOWN SWEETHEARTS:
Small towns, huge passion

Dear Reader,

I met Liam and Ellie while writing *The Marine's Secret Daughter* and looked forward to telling their story. It wasn't until I started writing that I realized their light banter hid some very deep emotions. As a writer, I love my characters, so torturing them wasn't easy, but I needed to peel back the layers to expose their pain so they could heal.

After surviving childhood cancer, Ellie Harding believes in grabbing on to life. So when she gets a chance to be with her longtime crush—who also happens to be her best friend's brother—she knows she could get her heart broken. What she didn't expect was to get pregnant...with twins!

After the loss of his mother and a colleague to cancer, Liam McBride knows the heartbreak the disease can cause, so he's fought his feelings for his little sister's friend. He steps up when Ellie becomes pregnant, but can he protect his heart?

If you've read my first two books in the Small-Town Sweethearts series, you'll recognize some familiar faces in *His Unexpected Twins*. But don't worry if you haven't read them because this one, like the others, is a stand-alone story.

I hope you enjoy Liam and Ellie's journey to a happy ending. Please join me later this year for a Christmas story set in Loon Lake, with a former naval aviator and the single mother who sees past the lieutenant's surly outer layer.

I love to hear from readers! Please visit my website: carrienichols.com.

Carrie Nichols

His Unexpected Twins

Carrie Nichols

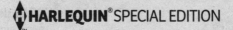

Recycling programs
for this product may
not exist in your area.

ISBN-13: 978-1-335-57403-9

His Unexpected Twins

Copyright © 2019 by Carol Opalinski

Printed in U.S.A.

Carrie Nichols grew up in New England but moved south and traded snow for central AC. She loves to travel, is addicted to British crime dramas and knows a *Seinfeld* quote appropriate for every occasion.

A 2016 RWA Golden Heart® Award winner and two-time Maggie Award for Excellence winner, she has one tolerant husband, two grown sons and two critical cats. To her dismay, Carrie's characters—like her family—often ignore the wisdom and guidance she offers.

Book by Carrie Nichols

Harlequin Special Edition

Small-Town Sweethearts

The Marine's Secret Daughter
The Sergeant's Unexpected Family

In loving memory of my cousin
Captain Donald "Chuck" Elliott
of the Springfield (MA) Fire Department.

Chapter One

"How about that new guy from—"

"No." Ellie Harding paused mid-slice in the sheet cake she was dividing into equal squares to scowl at her friend's attempts at matchmaking.

Meg McBride Cooper stood on the opposite side of the rectangular table, a stack of plain white dessert plates cradled against her chest. Ellie and Meg were volunteering at the payment-optional luncheon held weekly in the basement of the whitewashed clapboard church on the town square in Loon Lake, Vermont.

"I don't need or want help finding a date," Ellie said, and considering what she'd survived in her twenty-seven years, going solo to a friend's wedding shouldn't even be a blip on her radar. Did her friends think she couldn't find a date on her own? Memories surfaced of how she'd sometimes been treated after her cancer diagnosis. She knew her friends didn't pity her, but experiencing being pitied behind her back as well as to her face as a child had made her more sensitive as an adult.

Ellie pushed aside memories and went back to slicing the chocolate frosted cake with vigorous strokes. Heck, guys called her. Yep. They called all the time. *Slice*. They called when they needed a shortstop for a pickup softball game or a bowling partner. *Slice*. One even called last month, asking if she had a phone number for that new X-ray tech. *Slice*.

Meg plopped the plates onto the table with a *thunk* and gnawed on her bottom lip as she gazed at Ellie. Yeah, Meg was feeling guilty and wanted to confess something.

"Spill it," Ellie ordered.

"Now, don't get mad, but…" Meg sighed. "I asked Riley if he knew anyone who might be interested in being your date for the wedding."

"Uh-oh. Is Meg trying to set you up with arrestees… again?" A fellow volunteer, Mary Carter, came to stand shoulder to shoulder with Ellie, another sheet pan clutched in her hands. Mary was the future bride in question and a transplant to their close-knit central Vermont community, but she had jumped into town life and activities with enthusiasm. "Really, Meg, don't you think Ellie can do better than a felon? I'm sure if I asked, Brody could contact one of his old army buddies. I'll tell him to only choose ones that have never been arrested."

Meg rolled her eyes. "I'm sure asking Brody won't be necessary, Mary."

"Just in case…" Mary set the cake next to the stack of plates. "Ellie, what are your feelings on speeding tickets, because—"

"Oh, for heaven's sake," Meg interrupted and made an impatient sound with her tongue.

Ellie stifled a giggle at their antics but couldn't decide if she was grateful or annoyed. Now that her two besties had found happily-ever-afters, they seemed to think it their sworn duty to get her settled, too. So what if she hadn't found Mr. Right yet? Between long shifts as a nurse in the ER and studying for a more advanced degree, she led a full, busy life, thank you very much.

Mary winked at Ellie. "At least *I'm* not trying to set her up with someone who's been arrested."

"As I've told both of you already, that guy wasn't under arrest." Meg planted her hands on her hips. "He just happened to be in the building and Riley recruited him for a police lineup, that's all there was to it. No crime. No arrest."

Ellie continued to slice the cake. "If there was no crime, why was there a police lineup?"

"I meant *he* didn't commit a crime."

Mary slanted a look at Ellie. "Please correct me if I'm wrong, but didn't the witness identify him?"

"Mary," Meg huffed. "You're not helping."

"Sorry," Mary said, but her grin told a different story.

Ellie sucked on her cheeks to stifle a laugh, grateful to be off the hot seat, even temporarily. She appreciated her friends' concern but she wasn't a project. At times like this, Meg conveniently forgot she hadn't dated anyone for five years until Riley Cooper came back to town after serving in the marines in Afghanistan. Ellie decided not to point that out because her friends meant well. And she didn't want to turn their attention—and matchmaking attempts—back to her.

Meg blew her breath out noisily, disturbing the wisps

of curly red hair that had escaped her messy ponytail. "I've explained this to you guys like a thousand times already. It was a case of mistaken identity. I swear."

"Uh-huh, sure." Mary laughed and elbowed Ellie. "Ooh, maybe Riley can get the sheriff's department to start an eligible bachelor catch-and-release program."

"You guys are the worst," Meg grumbled, and began laying out the plates.

"Yup, the absolute worst, but you love us, anyway." Ellie grinned as she plated cake slices.

"Yeah, it's a good thing— Ooh, Ellie, how about that oh-my-God-he's-so-gorgeous guy coming down the stairs? If I wasn't hopelessly in love with Brody..." Mary bumped shoulders with Ellie and motioned with head.

Ellie's gaze followed Mary's and her heart stuttered. *Liam McBride.* What was he doing at the luncheon? She'd had a serious crush on Meg's brother since...well, since forever. At four years older, Liam had seen her as an annoying kid and had treated her accordingly. By the time she'd matured enough for him to notice, she'd been "his kid sister's friend" for so long she doubted it registered that she was a grown woman.

"What? Who? Where?" Meg whirled around and made a sound with her tongue against her teeth. "That's Liam."

"Liam?" Mary's eyes widened. "You mean that's—"

"Ellie's date for the wedding." Meg swiveled back, clapping her hands together, her mouth in a wide smile. "It's perfect."

"What? No." Ellie took a step back, shaking her head and holding up the knife as if warding off marauding zombies. She could accept matchmaking between friends. Even being relegated to Liam's friend zone would be acceptable, but begging for a pity date? *Nuh-uh*. Not gonna happen. No way. "Absolutely not."

"No… *No?*" Mary glanced at Liam again and snapped back to Ellie, looking at her as if she were insane for refusing. "I don't know why you wouldn't want—"

"Because he's Meg's brother." Ellie sneaked another glance at the sexy six-foot-two hunk of firefighter strutting toward them.

From his chronically disheveled dark brown hair and broad shoulders to his slim hips, long legs and that touch of confident swagger, Liam McBride oozed pheromones. And Ellie longed to answer their alluring call by throwing herself at his feet, but good sense, not to mention strong self-preservation instincts, prevailed. Thank God, because she didn't relish getting stepped on by those size 13 Oakley assault boots. To him, she was his little sister's friend. The girl who used to make moon eyes at him, the teen who blushed and stuttered every time he talked to her. When she'd been diagnosed with cancer in her teens, one of her first thoughts had been that she might never get to kiss Liam McBride.

"Be right back," Meg threw over her shoulder and rushed to meet her brother as he crossed the room.

"Oh, my. I mean, I had no idea," Mary whispered, leaning closer to Ellie. "Whenever she mentioned her brother, I was picturing a male version of Meg. You know…vertically challenged, wild red hair, freckles."

Ellie burst out laughing, but drew in a sharp breath when Liam's head snapped up. His gaze captured hers and his lips quirked into an irresistible half grin. The air she'd sucked in got caught in her chest. Why did he have to be so damn sexy? As if handsomeness had been handed out unchecked on the day he received his looks.

"Liam takes after their dad," she whispered to Mary. And not just in physical appearance.

Ellie knew Liam and his dad had buried themselves in work when Bridget McBride got sick. Firefighting was an admirable profession, but relationships needed care and feeding, too. All Ellie had to do was look at her parents to understand the cost when one partner checked out emotionally during a life-threatening situation. She might have survived the cancer that had plagued her childhood, but her parents' close relationship hadn't. As an adult she knew the guilt she'd carried throughout her teen years was irrational, but that didn't stop it from gnawing at her whenever she saw her parents together. What happened to them proved no relationship was immune to life's challenges.

So she'd admire the sexy firefighter, and if given the chance, she'd take that secret Make-A-Wish kiss, but she'd keep her heart and hopes for the future far, far away from Liam McBride.

"Heart? You listening?" she asked sotto voce before sneaking another longing glance at Liam.

Liam's footsteps had faltered at that distinctive laugh. *Ellie Harding.* Her laughter, like her honey-brown eyes, sparkled and drew him in whenever she was close. Today, her long, shiny dark hair was pulled back and secured with one of those rubber band thingies his sister and niece favored. He shook his head and tried to force his thoughts into safer territory. As his sister's friend, Ellie was off-limits, a permanent resident of the no-dating zone. It was a good thing they lived three hours apart so he wasn't faced with temptation on a regular basis. The last time he'd seen her was at his nephew's christening, nearly nine months ago.

The fact that she'd had cancer as a child and could have died had nothing to do with his resistance to her charms. Nothing at all. He'd hate to think he was that shallow, despite knowing the destruction illness left in its wake.

No. His reluctance was because messing with a sibling's friend could have nasty consequences. He and his best friend, Riley Cooper, were just patching up a huge rift in their friendship. Riley had broken the bro code and Liam's trust by getting Meg pregnant before deploying to Afghanistan and disappearing from her life. But all that was in the past. His sister was crazy in love with Riley, who'd come back, taken responsibility for his daughter and convinced Meg to marry him. Riley was also the reason for the glow of happiness in his sister's eyes these days.

So he'd buried the hatchet, and not in Riley's privates as he'd longed to do once upon a time. He was even spending saved vacation time in Loon Lake to help his brother-in-law renovate. Meg and Riley were outgrowing their modest cottage-style home after the birth of their second child, James.

His gaze met Ellie's and objections scattered like ashes. Damn, but off-limits would be a lot easier if she weren't so appealing. Why some guy hadn't scooped her up by now was a mystery. He almost wished one had and removed temptation. *Almost*. Something he kept buried deep and refused to explore railed against the picture of Ellie married to a random dude, forever out of reach. Except out of reach was where she needed to stay, because he'd filled his quota of losing people. From here on out, his heart belonged to his job. *Stay back three hundred feet, Ellie Harding.*

"Liam, what are you doing here?" Meg asked.

"I'm here to help Riley with your addition, remember?"

"I mean here…at the luncheon."

"When you weren't home, I remembered you volunteered here on Thursdays." He shrugged. "So, here I am."

She grinned and looped her arm through his. "You have no idea what perfect timing you have."

Then she began guiding—yeah, more like frog-marching—him across the church basement toward Ellie of the twinkling eyes and engaging laugh.

Liam's indrawn breath hissed through his teeth. "Uh-oh."

"You're the answer to our problem," Meg said in a too-bright tone, and squeezed his arm.

"Huh, that's new." He gave her a side-eye look. "Usually you're accusing me of being or causing the problem."

Meg's expression was calculating, as if sizing him up for something. *Crap.* He knew that look and nothing good ever came from it. Now that she was happily married, she seemed to think everyone should be. Living three hours away, he'd managed to avoid her less-than-subtle hints that it was time he settled down. He loved his sister and was happy to help with the interior finishing work on her new home addition, but he wasn't about to let her manipulate him into any sort of permanent relationship. Even if the intended target had the most beautiful golden eyes he'd ever seen.

He made a show of looking around. "Where's Riley? Why isn't your husband here solving your problems? Isn't that what he's for?"

"Nah, he can't help with this one, so enjoy being the solution for once, brother dear." Meg stopped at the table where Ellie and an attractive dark-haired woman about the same age were dishing out slices of chocolate cake.

"Meg tells me you need me to sample that cake." He winked at Ellie, who blushed. His breath quickened at her flushed features. *Friend zone*, he repeated to himself, but his mind kept conjuring up unique and enjoyable ways of keeping that pretty pink color on her face.

Meg tugged on his am, acting like her seven-year-old daughter, Fiona. "First, agree to our proposition, then you can have cake."

Ellie was shaking her head and mouthing the word *no*. Obviously whatever Meg had in mind involved her. Despite his wariness, he was intrigued.

Meg was nodding her head as vigorously as Ellie was shaking hers. "Ellie needs a date for Mary's wedding."

"I do not. Don't listen to her. This was all your sister's harebrained idea." Ellie dumped a piece of cake onto a plate and it landed frosting side down. She cursed and he cleared his throat to disguise his laugh.

"But Liam is going to be in town, so it's perfect," Meg said.

He winced. Tenacious was Meg's middle name. Another reason to keep Ellie in that friend zone. He'd have to live with the fallout into eternity.

"Hi, I'm Mary. The bride." The raven-haired woman set aside the slice with the frosting side down and thrust out her hand. "And you're welcome to come to my wedding with—" she glanced at Ellie "—or without a date."

He untangled his arm from Meg's and shook hands. "Thanks, I—"

"Oh, look. They need help at the pay station," Meg said, and scooted away.

"Nice meeting you, Liam. I'd love to stay and chat, but I promised to help in the kitchen." Mary disappeared as quickly and efficiently as his sister.

"Cowards," Ellie muttered, and shook her head. "Look, I'm not hitting you up to be my date for the wedding. I'm fine going by myself."

He nodded. Ellie was smart and independent, but that didn't mean she wanted to go to a wedding alone if everyone else was paired up. They could go as friends. And if he happened to hold her close as they danced… He shook his head, but the image of Ellie in his arms wouldn't go away. Huh, Meg wasn't the only tenacious person today. And damn if Meg hadn't once again manipulated him. "Are you saying you don't want to go with me? I've been known to behave myself in public."

Ellie raised her eyebrows, but her eyes glinted with mischief. "That's not what I've heard."

"Lies and exaggerations. Don't believe a word you hear and only half of what you see." He pulled a face.

"Uh-huh, sure." She laughed and went back to dishing out cake.

Her laugh washed over him and he arranged the plates so the empty ones were closer to her. People had begun lining up at the other end of the string of tables, but no one had reached the dessert station yet. He took advantage and hurried to Ellie's side of the table. He could help hand out the cake. Yeah, he was a regular do-gooder and it had nothing to do with standing next to Ellie and breathing in her light, flowery scent. "Why don't you want to go to this wedding with me?"

Ellie shook her head. "I'm not looking for a pity date."

He sighed. If she knew where his thoughts had been, she wouldn't be saying that. Besides, it wasn't like a real date because they'd be friends hanging out together. As simple as that. "So how do I appeal to your better nature and get you to take pity on me?"

"What? No. I meant…" she sputtered, her face turning pink again. She made what sounded like an impatient noise and put the last slice of cake on a plate.

He shouldn't, but he enjoyed seeing her flustered and if he was the cause, all the better, because she certainly had that effect on him. "How did you do that?"

She looked up and frowned. "Do what?"

He could get lost in those eyes. *Focus, McBride.* He cleared his throat and pointed to the last cake square on the plate. "You made those come out even."

A smile spread across her face and she glanced around before leaning close. "It's my superpower."

"I'm intrigued," he whispered, but he wasn't referring to cake or plates.

She straightened and turned her attention to a woman who appeared in front of them. "Hello, Mrs. Canterbury. Cake?"

After the woman had taken her cake and left, he bumped his hip against Ellie's. "Whaddaya say, Harding, help a guy out. Do your good deed for the month and come to this wedding with me?"

She narrowed her eyes at him. "Why? So I can perform CPR on the women who faint at your feet?"

Liam threw his head back and laughed. He spotted

Meg watching them, a smug expression on her face. He'd deal with his sister later. Maybe he could interest Fiona in a drum set or buy James, who would be walking soon, a pair of those annoying sneakers that squeaked.

Except he was intrigued by the idea of going with Ellie, so he gave her what he hoped was his best puppy-dog face. "Please. I hear it's the social event of the season."

"Oh, brother," she muttered and rolled her eyes.

Why had it suddenly become so important for her to say yes? He should be running the other way. Ellie didn't strike him as the sort of woman who did casual, and that's all he was looking for—with Ellie or anyone. Keep it light. No more wrenching losses. But that damn image of holding her while dancing, their bodies in sync, sometimes touching, wouldn't go away.

"How long are you staying in Loon Lake?"

Her question dragged him away from his thoughts and he frowned. "Exactly when is this wedding?"

"You missed the point. That was my attempt at changing the subject," she said, and greeted an elderly woman shuffling past.

Liam smiled at the woman and tried to hand her a dessert.

The woman shook her head and held up a plate loaded with meat loaf, potatoes and green beans. "Gotta eat this first, son."

Liam nodded, put the dessert back on the table and turned his head to Ellie. "I'll be here for a month."

"Goodness gracious, son, it won't take me that long to eat," the woman said before meandering off to find a seat.

Ellie giggled, her eyes sparkling with amusement, and he couldn't look away. *She's Meg's friend. Are you forgetting about cancer and how much it hurts to lose someone?* Sure, she was in remission, but there was a reason that term was used instead of *cured.* In his mother's case, the remission didn't last. Ellie was off-limits for so many reasons. But that message was getting drowned out. "So, you'll go with me to this wedding?"

"Look, Liam, I appreciate the offer, but—"

He leaned closer, dragging in her scent, and tilted his head in the direction of his sister. "It might shut her up for a bit. Let her think she got her way."

"Hmm." Ellie sucked on her lower lip for a second, then shook her head. "Nah. It'll just encourage her."

"It'll throw her off the scent if we hang out for a bit. We'll know that's all we'd be doing, but she won't." He'd lost his ever-lovin' mind. Yup, that must be the explanation for pursuing such an idiotic suggestion.

Ellie smiled and continued to hand out the cake. Although she had fewer freckles than she had as a kid, she still had a sprinkling of them high on her cheekbones and the bridge of her nose. He wouldn't have thought freckles could be sexy, but on Ellie they were, and he had to fight the urge to count them by pressing his fingertips to each one. Or better yet, his tongue.

"But we won't really be dating?" she asked during a lull in the line of people.

"Did you want to date?" What the hell was he doing asking such a loaded question? He handed out the last piece of cake to an elderly man in a Red Sox baseball cap.

"Meg means well, but it might be nice to take a break

from her matchmaking efforts." She picked up the plate with the frosting-side-down slice and held it up. "Split?"

"Sure." He reached for the fork she offered. His fingers brushed hers as he took the utensil and their gazes met. "Thanks. Looks delicious."

Her cheeks turned pink, making the tiny freckles stand out even more. As if they were begging for someone—him—to run their tongue along them. He cleared his throat and jabbed his fork in the cake.

"So, whaddaya say, Harding, do we have a deal?"

She shrugged. "Sure, McBride, why not?" Someone called her name and she turned away to leave but said over her shoulder, "We'll talk."

He set the fork on the empty plate and watched her disappear into the kitchen. She never did answer his question about wanting to date. Not that it mattered, because they would be hanging out. No dating. No relationship. Nice and safe: the way he preferred it.

Chapter Two

"Check out the guy who just walked in." Stacy, the triage nurse on duty, elbowed Ellie.

Ellie looked up from the notes she'd been studying to glance out the large glass window into the emergency waiting area. Her heart sped at the sight of Liam dressed in jeans and a dark blue Red Sox championship T-shirt approaching them. She hadn't seen him since the community luncheon two days prior, but he hadn't been far from her thoughts. If Stacy hadn't spotted him first, Ellie might have wondered if he was figment of her overactive imagination.

Ignoring Stacy's obvious curiosity, Ellie opened the door to the triage area. "Hey, what are you doing here?"

"Hey, yourself." He gave her that sexy half grin that threatened to leave her in a puddle.

Janitorial, mop up triage, please.

She clutched the clipboard across her chest as if it could protect her vital organs like a lead apron during X-rays. "Everything okay?"

"Heard you'd be getting off soon." He shrugged. "Thought you might like to grab some supper with me."

In the little office, Stacy cleared her throat, but Ellie ignored her.

Was he asking her on a date? "And where did you hear my shift was ending?"

"I asked Meg." He put his hands into his front pockets and hunched his shoulders forward. "So, how about some supper?"

A pen dropped, followed by a sigh. Stacy was probably memorizing every word and detail of the encounter to pass along later in the cafeteria.

Ellie shuffled her feet. Was she going to do this? *Repeat after me: "not a real date."* "Sure. I've got some extra clothes in my locker. If you don't mind waiting while I change."

From the sound of it, Stacy was rearranging files on her desk, and evidently, they were fighting back.

Ellie grinned and turned around. "Stacy, have you met my friend Meg Cooper's brother, Liam?"

Stacy stepped forward and stuck out her hand. "Pleased to meet you, Liam."

"Let me get changed. I'll be right back," Ellie said while Stacy and Liam shook hands.

Stacy laughed. "Don't rush on my account."

Despite Stacy's comment, Ellie hurried to her locker. Had this been Liam's idea or was Meg somehow behind this? After changing into jeans and a short-sleeved cotton sweater, she undid her hair from the braid and brushed it out. Even if this wasn't an honest-to-goodness date, she wanted to look her best. She fluffed her hair around her shoulders and applied some cherry lip gloss and went in search of Liam.

Hands shoved in his back pockets, Liam stood in front of the muted television in the waiting area. He turned as she approached and smiled broadly. "I gotta say, Harding, you clean up nicely."

"Not so bad yourself, McBride." She put her purse strap over her shoulder and waved to Stacy through the window. The triage nurse was with a patient but glanced at Liam and back to Ellie with a grin and a thumbs-up.

"I thought we'd take my truck and I can bring you back here for your car," Liam said as the automatic doors slid open with an electronic *whoosh*.

A light breeze was blowing the leaves on the trees surrounding the parking lot. A thunderstorm earlier in the day had broken the heat and humidity, making the evening warm but comfortable.

"Sounds good." *Sounds like a date.*

Using his key fob to unlock his truck, he approached the passenger side and opened the door for her. "Riley says that new hard cider microbrewery on the town square has great food."

"They do. Best burgers in town, if you ask me." She sucked on her bottom lip as she climbed into his truck. Everyone in Loon Lake knew Hennen's Microbrewery was the place to hang out with friends, while Angelo's was the restaurant you brought your date to. So, not a date. *At least we cleared that up.*

Once she was in the passenger seat, he shut the door and strolled around the hood of the truck. He climbed in and settled himself behind the wheel.

"Yeah, Meg mentioned that Angelo's has added a

dining patio but—" He started the truck and music from the Dropkick Murphys blasted from the speakers. Leaning over, he adjusted the volume. "Sorry about that."

His movements filled the front seat with his signature scent. She was able to pick out notes of salty sea air, driftwood and sage. Thinking about his aftershave was better than trying to figure out what he'd been about to say about Angelo's. Okay, color her curious. "You were saying something about Angelo's new patio."

He checked the mirrors and the backup camera before leaving the parking spot. "Hmm…oh, yeah. Meg said during the winter you can see across the lake to their house from the patio."

Serves you right for asking. "That's cool."

He cleared his throat. "She was going on and on about how romantic the new patio was with something called fairy lights."

Not exactly subtle, Meg. Ellie fiddled with the strap of her purse. "Yeah, they've got small trees in ceramic pots scattered around with tiny LED lights strung around the trunks and branches. Very pretty, with lots of atmosphere."

The air in the confined space felt supercharged with something…awareness? Chemistry? She couldn't be sure, couldn't even be sure that he felt it, too. Maybe this was all in her head. All one-sided, like it had been in her childhood.

He glanced at her for a second before bringing his attention back to the road. "So, you've been to Angelo's patio?"

Was he trying to get information on her social life or lack thereof? "No, but Mary and Meg have both been."

She huffed out her breath. "Believe me, I've heard all about it."

He reached over and laid his hand over hers. "Sounds like I may have to take up the challenge to be sure you get to experience this patio, too."

Her heart did a little bump, but she laughed, hoping to brazen through. "You signing me up as their new janitor, McBride?"

He squeezed her hand and brought it to his chest. "You wound me, Harding. I was thinking more along the lines of the waitstaff. I can see you in a white blouse and a cute little black skirt."

"Glad we cleared that up." She laughed for real this time. Date or not, there was no reason she couldn't enjoy being with Liam. Even if anything that could happen with Liam had nowhere to go. They didn't live in the same town. And then there was the whole thing with Liam having used his job to avoid dealing with his emotions. Even his sister couldn't deny that truth. But that didn't mean she couldn't enjoy hanging out with him while he was here. Having a life-threatening illness like lymphoma had taught her she didn't want to die with regrets if she could help it. After enduring chemo coupled with radiation, she'd been in remission for almost nine years, a good chunk of time, and her oncologist was optimistic but the experience had changed her outlook on life.

"How are the renovations coming?" she asked.

He squeezed her hand and put it back on her lap. "Is this you changing the subject?"

"So you *can* take a hint."

He jokingly muttered something about respect for her elders but launched into an amusing story about framing out the new master bedroom closet at Meg and Riley's place.

"That house is going to be awesome once the addition is finished."

He made a hum of agreement. "Yeah, I guess she made the right choice moving here."

"She said you had tried to get her to move into one of your rentals." She hadn't seen Liam's place, but she knew he owned one of those iconic Boston three-family homes commonly referred to as "three-deckers" by the locals. He'd purchased it as a bank foreclosure and had been remodeling it ever since, according to Meg. Ellie knew it was Liam's pride and joy.

"I did, but she's always loved this town and that vacation home. Even all the repairs it needed didn't deter her. My sister can be stubborn."

Ellie laughed. "Yeah, so I noticed."

"But I gotta say, she made the right choice for her." He stopped for a red light.

"What about you?" The words were out before she could prevent them.

He turned his head to look at her. "Me? I'm exactly where I belong."

Yeah, that's what she thought. And like Meg, he was happy where he lived.

Swallowing, she pointed out the windshield. "Green light."

She glanced at Liam's strong profile. Could *she* be happy in Boston? "No regrets" included trying new things, new places.

Hey, Ellie, aren't you getting a little ahead of yourself? This wasn't even a real date.

The route along Main Street took them past a few rectangular, early-nineteenth-century gable-roofed houses gathered around the town green. Some of the stately homes had been repurposed as doctors' offices, an insurance agency and an attorney's office, but some were still single-family residences.

The manicured common space boasted a restored white gazebo that doubled as a bandstand for concerts and picnics in the summer. Homes soon gave way to brick-fronted businesses, and the white Greek Revival church where they held the weekly lunches. With its black shutters and steeple bell tower, the church anchored the green at one end.

No doubt the town was picturesque, but she recalled how, when she was sick, the women of Loon Lake had worked year-round to keep the Hardings' refrigerator full of casseroles and sandwich fixings. In the summer, the men had made sure their lawn was mowed. In the winter, the men plowing for the town had been careful to keep the end of their driveway relatively clear.

He pulled the truck into one of the angled parking spots in front of the pub-style restaurant. "I'm assuming you've been here before, since you said you liked the burgers."

"Yeah, I've been a few times with some of the people from work."

He turned the engine off and opened his door. Ellie opened hers and was getting out when he came around to her side. He put his hand under her elbow to steady her as she scrambled out. His touch sent sparks up her arm…straight to her core.

You'd better be listening, she cautioned her heart. *Liam and I are hanging out, nothing more.* Unlike Angelo's, this wasn't a romantic date place. Since this wasn't a date, she had no right to feel disappointed. And she certainly had no right to be using or thinking the word *romantic* in context with anything she and Liam did.

They strolled across the sidewalk to the entrance, his hand hovering over the small of her back, not quite touching. How was she supposed to read the mixed signals he was sending? Maybe it was all her fault for trying to read things into his actions and words that weren't there. *Your fault because you wanted this to be a date and it's a let's-hang-out night.* She swallowed the sigh that bubbled up.

He turned his head toward her as they made their way toward the restaurant. "Something wrong with Hennen's?"

Had he picked up on her confusion? She shook her head. "No. It's fine."

"Hey, I'm not such a guy that I don't know what 'fine' in that tone of voice means." He held the glass entry door open.

After stepping inside, she glanced up at him, her eyebrows raised. "And what does 'fine' mean?"

The outer door shut, leaving them alone in the restaurant's vestibule. A small table with a bowl of wrapped mints and stack of takeout menus stood off to one side. Muffled sounds—music, conversations and clinking of dishware—came from beyond the inner door.

"I'm thinking it means there's something wrong and I'm expected to figure it out." His light blue eyes darkened.

Lost in those eyes, she had to swallow before she could speak. "And have you figured it out?"

"No, but I have an idea how to fix it." He took a step toward her, his intense gaze on her lips.

"Oh? You can fix it without even knowing what it is?" All thoughts of why she was even upset flew out of her head. Liam's sexy and oh-so-kissable lips took up all available space.

"Uh-huh," he said, and lowered his head. "I was thinking of kissing it and making it all better."

She noisily sucked in her breath. Were they really going to do this? Here of all places?

"Are you in?" His voice was hoarse, his expression hopeful as his gaze searched hers.

She rose on her tiptoes, placed her hands on either side of his face, pulling him close enough she smelled breath mints. "Does this answer your question?"

He dipped his head until his lips latched onto hers. The kiss was gentle, probing but firm. Her sigh parted her lips and his tongue slipped inside. The kiss she'd been waiting for her entire life was even better than she'd thought possible. It was sexy enough to send heat to her most sensitive areas and yet sweet enough to bring tears to her eyes. *Make-A-Wish, eat your heart out.*

She wanted it to last forever, but cooled air and noise from the restaurant blasted them as the inner door opened. Someone cleared their throat and Liam pulled away so quickly she swayed. His hands darted out, coming to rest around each side of her waist and lingering for a moment before dropping away.

"Ellie?" a familiar voice inquired.

Liam stepped aside and she came face-to-face with Brody Wilson. She groaned inwardly. As if getting caught kissing in public wasn't embarrassing enough, it had to be by someone she knew, someone who would tell his fiancée, Mary, who would tell Meg. Trying to salvage the situation, Ellie plastered a smile on her face, which was probably as red as the ketchup on the tables inside.

"This is, uh…a surprise." She turned toward Liam. "Have you two met?"

Brody juggled a large white paper bag into the other hand, then reached out to shake. "We met very briefly at Meg and Riley's wedding."

"Speaking of weddings, you must be the groom." Liam shook hands. "I met the bride a couple days ago."

"Yes, Mary mentioned that." Brody nodded, his assessing gaze darting between them.

"Are Mary and Elliott with you tonight?" Ellie glanced through the glass door to the restaurant.

"No. They're at home." He held up the bag. "I stopped to grab burgers on my way back from checking in on Kevin Thompson."

"Checking on Kevin?" Ellie touched Brody's arm. "Did something happen?"

Kevin Thompson was a local youth who could have headed down the wrong path if not for Loon Lake's caring residents. Ellie knew Riley and Meg had encouraged Kevin to stay in school, and Brody and Mary had boosted his self-confidence by having him interact with the kids at their summer camp for children in foster care.

The camp had been Mary's dream. When she and Brody became a couple, they'd started a nonprofit and made her dream a reality. Their farm on the edge of town was the perfect spot.

Brody nodded. "Yeah, he sprained his wrist yesterday."

"Oh, no. Wasn't he your helper for the carnival preparations?"

Brody sighed. "With Riley working on their house and picking up overtime hours, I hate to ask him, but I may have to if we're going to be ready on time."

Liam quirked an eyebrow at her. "What's this about a carnival?"

"I help out with a childhood cancer survivor group," Ellie said. "We counsel survivors and those going through treatment. Plus, every year we put on a carnival as a fun activity for the kids." She enjoyed giving back to a group that had been so helpful when she'd needed it. "We have as much fun as the kids and it's important for them to see they can get through sometimes grueling treatments and enjoy life."

"What sort of help do you need?" Liam asked Brody.

Brody stroked his chin with his free hand. "Mostly muscle and someone to assemble wooden booths. You good with a hammer?"

Liam bobbed his head once. "Sure. I'd be happy to help out."

The inner door opened and Brody stepped aside to let a couple pass through. "Ellie, why don't I give you a call later and we can make arrangements."

"That sounds good. You might want to get home before those burgers get cold or you'll be in trouble with Mary."

"Yeah, we don't want that." Brody laughed and winked.

Liam's hand found the small of Ellie's back as if magnetized. He licked his lips at the cherry taste that lingered on them. What had he been thinking, kissing her like that in public? Yeah, no thinking involved. Ellie's presence tended to scramble his thought process.

A hostess inside the restaurant greeted them and led them to a booth.

"Thank you for offering to help out with the carnival," Ellie said as she slid into the seat. "You're here working with Riley and now spending off-time working some more. Hardly seems fair."

He sat across from her. "Are you going to be there?"

"Yeah. I always help out," she said, and picked up the colorful menu.

Normally he'd run a mile from reminders of the disease that claimed his ma. Just thinking about cancer made his skin crawl, but he could man up and do this. For Ellie. "Then I'm in."

She gave him a big smile and flipped open the menu. Yeah, that smile was worth giving up a few hours to help some kids. He should regret the kiss but he didn't, couldn't regret something that felt so damn good. With that kiss, tonight felt more like a date, despite him being careful not to turn it into one.

He'd decided to keep things casual with Ellie because being in remission was no guarantee the cancer couldn't return. Nothing like wanting his cake and eating it, too, or in this case, wanting his Ellie and none of the burdens of a real relationship. How the hell was he going to make this work?

"Do you want to?"

Ellie's question brought him back with a jolt. Had he said any of that aloud? "Huh?"

She *tsk*ed. "I asked if you wanted to split an appetizer."

Before he could answer, someone called her name. Two men in EMT uniforms approached their booth. Liam frowned at the way they strutted over to Ellie's side. The tall one appeared to be around Ellie's age, while the shorter, dark-skinned one was older.

"Sorry, Ellie, we didn't mean to interrupt your date," said the older one.

She glanced over at Liam. "Oh, we're just—"

"On a date but it's no problem." What the hell prompted him to say that? He was still striving for control, for keeping his feelings casual. If they'd run into two of Ellie's female friends, would he have made the same claim? If he were a better man he'd know the answer. Since he didn't, that put him in the "not a better man" category.

"We're not staying, just picking up our supper, and noticed you in here while we were waiting," said the younger guy.

"I'm glad you came to say hi," Ellie said. "This is my friend Liam. Liam, this is Mike and Colton. As you can plainly see by their uniforms, they're EMTs. It just so happens Liam is a firefighter."

Liam shook hands with both men, applying a bit of pressure with the younger one, Colton, whose intense gaze had been on Ellie since they'd come over to the table. Yeah, more juvenile than a better man would behave, that's for sure.

"We missed you at the softball game last weekend," Colton said to Ellie, but gave Liam the once-over as he said it, as if Liam had prevented Ellie from playing.

Ellie rested her elbows on the table, lightly clasping her hands together. "Sorry I missed it. Did you win?"

"No. We got clobbered." Colton shook his head and scowled. "That's why we need you."

Mike backhanded his partner on the arm. "Looks like our order's up."

Colton nodded but didn't take his eyes off Ellie. "The cops challenged us to another game to raise money for a K-9 unit. You in?"

"Sure." Ellie smiled and nodded. "Give me a call when you get a time and place."

Liam bit down on the urge to tell the guy to get lost already. If Colton was interested, why hadn't *he* taken her to the new patio at Angelo's? *Pot? Kettle. You brought her here instead of trying to get reservations at Angelo's.*

"Some of the guys were talking about getting a bowling night together." Colton mimed holding a phone. "I'll give you call."

"Hey, man, you can't pick her up while she's on a date with someone else," Mike said, and attempted to pull his partner away from the table.

"Sheesh, I wasn't picking her up, just asking if she was interested in bowling. It's for charity," he grumbled, but turned back and grinned at Ellie. "See ya, Els."

Els? What the…? Liam ground his back teeth as the two EMTs walked away. "He was definitely trying to pick you up."

Ellie rolled her eyes. "Yeah, right. Colton called a couple months ago asking if I had the number of the new X-ray tech."

So this Colton was a player? Well, he could go play in someone else's sandbox. He and Ellie were…what? Hanging out to get Meg off their case did not a relationship make.

"Believe me, he was hitting on you," Liam insisted.

She glanced over at the two men leaving the restaurant.

"Maybe it didn't work out with the X-ray tech," Liam muttered, and shook the menu open with a snap.

"Maybe." She shrugged and set her menu down.

Did she have feelings for this Colton? He pretended to be interested in the menu's offerings. "That Mike guy—"

"Stop right there. You're not going to try to tell me he was hitting on me." She heaved a deep sigh. "Mike's happily married. He has a beautiful wife and two sweet daughters, all of whom he adores."

Before he could say anything more about either EMT, a petite waitress with a short blond bob and an eyebrow piercing came over to the table.

"Hi, I'm Ashley, and I'll be your server tonight," she said, and rested her hand on the table near his.

"I'll have a bacon cheeseburger and onion rings," Ellie told the waitress.

Ashley nodded and scribbled on her pad without taking her eyes off him. He echoed Ellie's order because he'd been too busy fending off her would-be suitor to read the menu.

"*Now* who is getting hit on?" Ellie said in a dry tone as she watched the perky blonde sashay across the room.

"Who? The waitress? She looks barely old enough to be serving drinks." He sipped his water. "And we were talking about you. Colton was definitely hitting on you."

She made a derisive sound blowing her breath through her lips. "I find that hard to believe."

He shook his head. Did she not know the effect she had on guys? That megawatt smile that made her eyes sparkle created a pull, one he couldn't deny. So why wouldn't any other guy feel the same? "What? Why would you say that?"

"Because guys don't see me like that. All they see

is a shortstop for their softball team or a bowler for charity."

"I don't know who put that idea in your head, but it's simply not true. And I'm a guy, so I should know." Damn. Why did he say that? If she liked this Colton dude, saying things like that might give her ideas.

She snorted. "I don't see you putting the moves on me."

"What if I were to put a move on you?"

"Yeah, right," she sputtered, and shook her head.

He let it drop, but began calculating how many moves he could make in thirty days.

Chapter Three

Several times during the day on Friday, Liam considered excuses to get out of helping Ellie with her carnival. Last weekend had been the anniversary of his mother's death from stage 3 breast cancer that had spread. The years had muted the pain, but he wasn't looking forward to all the reminders because it also reminded him of his friend and mentor, Sean McMahan. During Liam's year as a probationary firefighter, Sean had taken him under his wing and they'd become close. Cancer had claimed Sean eighteen months after Bridget McBride. And yet he couldn't—wouldn't—let Ellie down, so that evening, he accompanied her to the church where they were setting up for the carnival. He'd insisted on giving her a ride when she mentioned meeting him there. Generosity didn't enter into his offer; ulterior motives did. He wanted to see if she'd planned on coming or going with that EMT Colton, but her eager acceptance of his offer reassured him.

Liam resisted reaching for Ellie's hand as they descended the stairs to the brightly lit basement. The place buzzed with the sounds of hammering, chatter and laughter. The scent of raw wood and paint permeated the air.

"I promised to paint some of the signs and to help Mary corral some of the younger kids. We're providing nursery services to our volunteers," Ellie said with a touch on his arm. "I'll talk to you later."

Brody waved Liam over and wasted no time putting him to work constructing a booth for one of the carnival games. Brody gave him a rough sketch of what it was supposed to look like. After helping with Meg and Riley's renovations, this would be a cinch.

As Liam got busy laying out the precut wood Brody had supplied, a towheaded boy of around ten came to stand next to him. The boy shuffled his feet but didn't speak.

Liam picked up the first pieces. "Hey, there, I'm Liam. What's your name?"

"Craig." The boy glanced at his paint-stained sneakers. "Are you Miss Ellie's fireman?"

The pencil in Liam's hand jumped and messed up the line he'd been marking. *Calm down. He's a kid asking a question, not making an observational statement.* "I'm a fireman."

The boy's gaze rested on Liam. "I always wanted to be one."

Liam's heart turned over at the look of wistfulness on the boy's face. Did this kid have cancer? Or was he one of the survivors? The boy's choice of words hadn't gone unnoticed. "Have you changed your mind about it?"

Craig shook his head. "Nah. But my mom gets a worried look on her face when I talk about becoming a fireman...like she wants me to pick something else. She's been like that ever since my cancer."

"You still have lots of time to decide what you want to be when you grow up." What the heck was he supposed to tell the kid? Liam glanced around but everyone was busy building or shooing young ones back into one of the side rooms being used as a nursery.

The boy shrugged. "Yeah, the doctors say I'm in remission, but my mom still worries."

Liam knew how the kid's mom felt. He worried about losing more people to cancer, including Ellie, but he couldn't say that to the boy. "Do you think you could help me get this put together? I could use the extra hands."

Craig's face lit up as he vigorously nodded his head. "I sure would."

"Okay." Liam handed him a peanut butter jar full of nails. "You can hand me the nails when I ask."

The kid looked disappointed so Liam rushed to explain. "That way, I don't have to stop and grab one each time. This will go a lot faster with your help. And I'll be happy to answer any questions you have about firefighting as we work."

Craig seemed to consider it. "I just wish my mom wouldn't get that scared look when I talk about being a fireman."

"Well, you're still a little young to join. Maybe by the time you're old enough, your mom will feel better about you becoming a firefighter."

"I hope so. Does your mom worry?"

Had Bridget McBride worried when he joined the fire department? If she had, she'd kept it hidden. Of course, following in his dad's footsteps may have made a difference. He honestly didn't know if she worried because she'd never said so. "She might have."

"My mom says it's dangerous." The boy pulled his mouth in on one side.

Liam put his hand out for a nail. "I won't lie and say it isn't, but that's why you attend the fire academy for rigorous training and learn all you can about the job before getting hired. Even after you get hired, you're on probation."

"Huh?"

Liam resisted the urge to ruffle Craig's hair. Chances are the kid would be insulted. "It means you're still learning from the older guys."

Craig carefully laid a nail on Liam's outstretched palm. "You gotta go to school to be a fireman?"

"You sure do. Lots to learn about fires and staying safe." He hammered the boards together. At least with firefighting you had training and were in control of the equipment. It wasn't as if you could train for cancer. And doctors and others were in charge of the equipment to fight it, leaving you helpless. "We do all that training so we know exactly what to do to make it less dangerous. I can talk to the crew here in Loon Lake and see about taking you on a tour of the fire station. Maybe see what it's like to sit in one of the rigs."

Craig pulled out another nail. "That would be awesome. Thanks."

Liam nodded. "Sure thing. I'll talk to some of the guys."

"Miss Ellie says you're in Boston." Craig scrunched up his face. "How come?"

Liam took the nail. "That where I live, and my dad and his dad before him were on the Boston Fire Department. That's why I joined up."

"My dad's a lawyer. Is your dad still a fireman?"

"No, he's retired." Even after several years, it still felt weird to say that. Liam always thought Mac would be one of those guys who stayed until they carried him out the door. Had his dad let Doris talk him into retirement? He liked his dad's new wife. It had been awkward at first, seeing him with someone other than his mom, but now he was glad they'd found happiness together.

"What about your mom? Can you ask her? Maybe she can talk to mine and tell her it's okay."

Liam shook his head and swallowed. "I'm afraid not, buddy. My mom died."

"Cancer?"

"Yeah."

The boy nodded, looking much older than he should have. "That's a—" He broke off and glanced around. "That sucks."

"It does." Liam bit back a laugh. What had the kid been about to say? He caught that because he'd had to watch his language around his niece, Fiona.

"But Miss Ellie says you can't live your life afraid because you had cancer or you wouldn't have a life."

Liam began cleaning up after Craig left. He'd have to track down some of the guys at the Loon Lake station and see if they could arrange something for Craig. Maybe even something for the boy's mom to set her mind at ease. Ellie had said how she'd had to fight her parents' need to smother and hover even after she'd been in remission for the golden five-year mark. Her words, as repeated by Craig, kept coming back to him. *You can't live your life afraid because you had cancer or you wouldn't have a life.*

"I wanted to thank you for pitching in." A deep voice behind him caught Liam's attention.

He turned to Brody Wilson. "Hey, man, no problem. Glad to help."

Brody chuckled. "And earning Ellie's gratitude probably doesn't hurt, either."

Liam couldn't deny he liked putting that light in Ellie's golden eyes. "Looks like you have your hands full." Liam tipped his chin toward the curly-haired toddler chasing another boy around under Mary's watchful eye. Earlier, Brody had been chasing after his active son.

"Yeah, Elliott's a handful. When he's not sleeping, he's full speed ahead. He has no neutral." Brody's love and pride were evident in his voice and the expression on his face as he watched his son.

Liam knew from Ellie that Brody had adopted Mary's young son from her previous relationship with his half brother, Roger, who had wanted nothing to do with the baby. Elliott may have been rejected by his biological father, but Brody's love for the boy was obvious. "He's got lots of space to work off that energy. Meg tells me you've got a lot going on out at your farm. Some sort of camp for foster kids to come and enjoy fresh air and animals."

Brody laughed. "Yeah, believe it or not, I had picked that particular place thinking I wanted quiet and isolation."

Liam didn't know much about Brody except what

he'd heard from Meg or Ellie. But the guy had been through some nasty stuff during his time in the army, so his wanting someplace to nurse wounds, even the unseen kind, was understandable. "Funny how that sometimes works. What happened?"

"Mary and Elliott happened." Brody's expression went all soft. "I know it sounds corny, but they made me want to do what I could to make this a better world."

Brody had that same look Riley got when he talked about Meg. Ha, maybe it was something in the Loon Lake water. "And so you started the camp?"

"Camp Life Launch started as Mary's idea, but I guess you could say I took it and ran with it. Some of the guys I served with in the army are pitching in and we've even talked about doing something for returning veterans who might want to help with the kids or simply be surrounded by nature. You'd be surprised how calming watching the night sky or a pair of alpacas snacking on carrots and enjoying the sunshine can be."

Liam nodded and an idea struck him. Something Craig had said. "Sounds like something these kids might benefit from, too. Ellie says it can be hard for them to just be children, even after the cancer is under control."

Brody wiped a hand over his mouth. "You might have something there. The older ones might even enjoy volunteering as counselors to younger ones, show 'em life-after-cancer stuff. Kevin and Danny, those two boys your sister and brother-in-law were helping out, have turned into a valuable resource helping with some of our youth campers. I'll definitely talk to Mary about it."

Just then, Brody's curly-haired boy toddled up to

Liam. "Alley-oop," he said, thrusting his arms up and balancing on his toes.

"Alley-oop?" Liam shook his head and looked to Brody for help.

Brody chuckled and ruffled his son's hair. "Sorry, big guy, I don't think Liam understands Elliott Speak."

The boy bounced on his toes. "Alley-oop, alley-oop."

Brody glanced at Liam and laughed. "He's saying 'Elliott, up.' He's asking you to pick him up."

"Oh, okay, that I can do." Liam bent down and picked up the smiling toddler. He settled Elliott on his hip. "Have you been trying to keep up with the other kids? I think James is more your speed since he's still new to this whole walking gig."

"Won't be long before James will be running around, too." Brody laughed as he leaned over and chucked his son's chin. "Mary and I have started discussing giving this guy a brother or sister. We've been immersed in getting Camp Life Launch going this past year but things are settling down."

"Alley Daddy." The boy bounced up and down in Liam's arms.

"Yeah, that's your dad." Liam hung on to the agile toddler. Warmth spread across his chest at the feel of the toddler's sturdy weight in his arms. Holding Elliott had him thinking of what it would be like to have his own family. "You want to go back to him now?"

Elliott gave Liam a grin and pointed. "Alley Daddy."

Liam handed him over to Brody and the toddler threw his arms around Brody's neck.

"Alley Daddy." The toddler rubbed his face on Brody's shirt.

"I sure am, big guy." Brody rubbed the boy's back and turned to Liam. "He hasn't mastered his name yet."

Liam laughed. "I just got Fiona to say Liam and now James is calling me Meem."

"Meg is practically glowing these days. I'm so glad to see her happily settled."

"Yeah, I guess Riley has been good for her."

"Well, I know Mary and Elliott are the best thing that's ever happened to me." Brody shook his head as if in wonderment. "And I have a feeling this camp will be, too. If you ever want to stop by, feel free. Although I can't promise we won't put you to work."

"I may just do that," Liam said. Brody had the same glow of happiness as Meg. Would he ever be so lucky as to find such contentment? An image of Ellie came to mind and even the specter of her cancer returning couldn't chase it away.

"Thanks again for all the help. You should come back on carnival night and see everyone enjoying all your hard work."

Brody strolled over to Mary, who waved to Liam. Brody said something to her and leaned down and gave her a kiss.

"Hey, I see you're fitting right in." Ellie came to stand next to him.

"Fitting in?"

"Talking to Craig. He's been wanting to meet you ever since I told him I knew a real live fireman." Ellie hooked her arm through his. "Of course I was referring to your dad, but I guess you'll do."

"Hey." He drew his brows together and scowled, but his lips twitched with the need to grin.

"Did he ask about the job?"

"Yeah. He said his mom was trying to talk him out of it, but he's kinda young for her to be worried already." Liam leaned down and filled his nose with her scent.

"Things change when kids get cancer, and his mom has had a tendency to hover since his diagnosis. Firefighting can be considered a dangerous job."

Sure, but unlike cancer, *he* was in charge. "Yeah, I told him about all the training and safety equipment. I'd love to try to set something up locally if he wanted to visit the firehouse."

"That's really sweet of you. Thanks." She squeezed his arm. "What were you and Brody talking about?"

"He was telling me about the summer camp they've set up at their farm. When he said they had youths who'd turned their lives around act as counselors, I suggested kids like Craig might be interested in something like that, too. Maybe even act as advisers or counselors to children still going through that."

Her eyes widened. "You did that?"

"Yeah, why?" He tried to shrug it off, but the fact that she seemed pleased made his stomach swoop like it had on the day he'd shed his probie status with the department.

"I think that's a great idea. Thanks so much for suggesting it to Brody." She gave him a strangely amused smile.

Warmth rose in his face. How could he have been so oblivious? "You've already suggested it to him?"

She patted his chest. "Doesn't mean it's not a great idea, and I appreciate you taking an interest."

He grunted. "Are you patronizing me?"

She looked genuinely hurt and he regretted his accusation.

"Absolutely not," she said before he could apologize. "Mary and Brody offered to give me a ride home so you won't have to go out of your way to take me back. Your sister's place is in the other direction."

"I brought you. I take you home," he said, and scowled.

"Okay." She checked her watch. "It's still early. How about if I make some popcorn and we watch a movie? That is, if…if you want to."

He draped an arm over her shoulder. "I'd love to."

Ellie tried to contain her excitement as Liam drove them to her place from the church. How was Liam supposed to see her as an adult if she acted and sounded like her teen self around him? She'd even been sitting on the steps to her place waiting for him when he picked her up. *Way to go*, she scolded herself. Except he'd said yes to popcorn and a movie. And now she probably had a big goofy grin on her face.

They pulled into her driveway and drove past a rambling log home more suited to *Architectural Digest* than Loon Lake. Although she hadn't been inside she knew the floor-to-ceiling windows in the back offered a breathtaking view of the lake. The motion-sensitive lights came on as Liam's truck approached the three-car garage where she rented the upstairs apartment. Despite living here for six months, she had yet to meet the absent owner of the impressive main house. Her rental was handled through a management company.

Liam pulled his truck next to her car. "Am I blocking anyone if I park here?"

"No. It's fine. The log home's owner is still absent."

He hopped out of his truck. "Who owns it?"

"That's the big Loon Lake mystery." She started up

the stairs to her apartment. Partway up, she turned to him. "There's a rumor it belongs to Thayer Jones, that ex-hockey player who grew up here. But no one really knows. Even Tavie Whatley doesn't know for sure."

Liam laughed. "Then it really is a mystery."

Warmth flowed through her at his laugh. "Yeah, I didn't think it was possible to do anything in this town without Tavie knowing all the details."

Seventysomething Tavie Whatley ran Loon Lake General Store and much of the town from her perch behind the cash register. She and her husband, Ogle, were not only fixtures in the community but the force behind many of its charitable endeavors. Brody jokingly called Tavie Loon Lake's benevolent dictator.

She unlocked her door and they entered her small but efficient kitchen. She loved the light gray bottom cabinets, porcelain farmhouse-style sink and open shelving above a wooden countertop. A breakfast bar divided the kitchen from the living area. Off the living room was a short hall leading to her bedroom and the bathroom.

"I'd give you a tour, but this is really it—other than the bedroom…" She cleared her throat. Why did showing Liam her bedroom feel so awkward? Her bed was made and there wasn't a stuffed animal in sight: an adult bedroom. Huh, did she want to avoid reminders she was an adult and old enough to be sexually active? "How about some popcorn?"

"Sounds good. Need help?"

"Thanks. I got it covered." She handed him the remote. "You pick something while I get it." She pulled out her glass microwave popcorn maker, glancing at him sprawled on her sofa. *Don't get any ideas*, she cautioned herself. They were hanging out, sitting together and watching a movie. She set the microwave timer and looked over at him again. She swallowed. When had her couch gotten so small?

Liam was flipping through the movies on her paid streaming subscription. "What do you feel like watching?"

"How about that new action movie with what's-his-name?"

He turned his head to give her one of his sexy half grins. "Are you psychic? That's the one I've been wanting to see."

She laughed. "Just another example of my superpowers."

The timer on the microwave dinged and she removed the glass popper. She poured the popcorn in the bowl and salted it. Handing Liam the bowl, she plopped down next to him.

"How about this one?" He clicked on a movie selection. "It's got what's-his-name in it."

She tossed a popped kernel at him, but he caught it in his mouth and grinned as he chewed. He set the bowl on the coffee table and leaned closer.

She couldn't be sure who moved first, but their lips found each other in a sweet kiss that held the promise of more. All thoughts of movies and actors flew out of her head. He angled his face closer and she—

The music for the movie startled her and she abruptly pulled away. "Sorry."

"I'm not," he said, brushing her hair off her cheek and tucking it behind her ear.

He leaned back on the couch and pulled her into his side. She cuddled next to him and tried to concentrate on the movie, but it wasn't easy with his body warm against hers and his luscious scent surrounding her.

As the credits rolled he set the empty popcorn bowl on the end table next to the couch and picked up a book that had been on the table.

"This looks like a textbook."

"Yeah, working on my advanced nursing degree."

He nodded. "So you can finally move away from Loon Lake?"

"What? Absolutely not." She wasn't about to abandon the people who'd been there for her and her family when they'd needed it. "I like living in Loon Lake."

He flipped through some of the pages. "Will you be able to use the new degree at the hospital?"

"I suppose I could, but they'll be breaking ground soon on a skilled nursing facility and I'm hoping to work as a nurse practitioner there. If I time it right, I will have my gerontology degree when they finish construction."

"Skilled nursing facility?"

Ellie grinned. "A nursing home."

"Is that nurse speak?" he asked and wiggled his eyebrows.

She rolled her eyes. "C'mon, you're not turned on by nurse speak, are you?"

"Only if you're the one speaking it." He put the book back and settled against the cushions. "Sounds like you have it planned out."

"I want to help the people I've grown up with. Give back to a community that gave so much to me. I haven't forgotten how everyone rallied around when I was sick." Damn. She hadn't meant to bring up the past like that. She glanced at him out of the corner of her eye.

When he didn't comment but put an arm around her shoulder, she relaxed against him. "What about you? I heard you're determined to follow in your dad's footsteps at the fire department."

He nodded. "That's the plan. I should hear if I made captain soon. My dad was one of the youngest captains and I'm hoping to follow suit."

"So we haven't convinced you yet that Loon Lake is a great place to live?" She tried to keep her tone light, but she needed to hear him say it so maybe her stupid heart would get the message.

"Are you kidding?" He shook his head as he toyed with her hair. "The Loon Lake firehouse is part time. If not for guys who are willing to work in the department on their days off from full-time jobs, Loon Lake FD would be an all-volunteer one."

"And that's bad why?" Her body tensed on behalf of the guys she knew who worked for the town.

"It's not bad. It's how most small towns are able to afford full-time protection," he said. "But it's not what I want."

She swallowed. Yeah, that's what she thought. Riley Cooper and Brody Wilson might have embraced small-town life, but Liam evidently didn't feel like he could do the same.

Chapter Four

Liam turned off his truck and grabbed a pizza box off the passenger seat before climbing out. It had been three days since he'd helped with her carnival. He glanced up at a curtain blowing in an open window in the upstairs apartment and inhaled a deep, satisfied breath. Ellie was in there.

Ellie had texted to thank him for arranging for Craig's visit to the firehouse in Loon Lake. When he replied, he'd suggested supper and she'd offered to cook for him. He'd responded that he knew she'd been on her feet all day in the ER and offered to bring pizza.

He was halfway up the stairs when her door opened and she stood silhouetted in the doorway. As if she'd been waiting for him, as if she'd been as eager to see him.

Don't make this more than it is, he cautioned himself. They were simply friends hanging out. Nothing more.

"Hey, there," she said, and grinned.

Dressed in a T-shirt and shorts that showcased her long, slender legs, she got his blood pumping.

He reached the small landing at the top of the stairs. She was barefoot and for some reason that had him struggling to drag in air. Who knew bare feet were sexy? To him, they'd previously only been necessary for walking. He stood mute in front of her, thinking about her purple-painted toenails until her welcoming smile slipped and her brows gathered into a frown.

Mentally kicking himself, he forced words past his dry lips. "Hey, yourself."

Yeah, a real smooth talker, McBride.

She held out her hands for the box. He passed it over but didn't let go of his end. Tugging the cardboard toward him brought her closer. He leaned over and gently brushed his lips against hers. After thinking about her all day, he couldn't resist and the kiss couldn't get out of hand with the box between them. He had this whole situation under control.

She sucked in air when they pulled apart. "Wha-what was that for?"

Yeah, what was that for? "It was meant as a greeting between two friends."

Something passed over her face, something he couldn't interpret and only noticed because he'd been staring at her.

"Well then, c'mon in…friend." She took the pizza and went inside.

He wiped his feet on her welcome mat before entering the kitchen. She set the pizza on the counter next to a bottle of wine and stood on her toes to reach up to grab plates from the open shelving. Her T-shirt rode up and revealed a swath of creamy skin above her butt. He picked up the bottle of wine to keep from reaching out and running his fingers along that exposed skin to see if it was as soft and smooth as it looked.

"I have beer in the fridge. If you prefer that over wine." She came down flat on her feet and tilted her head toward the stainless steel refrigerator.

"Thanks. I prefer beer." He forced himself to look away.

She set the plates on the counter and pulled her shirt back down. "A cheap date. Nice to know."

"Me, cheap?" He picked up the wine again. "Ellie, this is two-buck Chuck."

"But it was such a good month." She set napkins on the plates.

He bumped shoulders. "We talkin' last month?"

"Pfft. And you're such a connoisseur?" She pushed back.

"Hey, I've been down the wine aisle at Whole Foods."

When she rolled her eyes, he leaned down and gave her a quick kiss on the end of her nose.

"Wha-what was that one for?"

"For being so impertinent." He licked his lips before continuing. "Now that we've gotten that out of the way, let's eat. I'm starved."

To hide the color he was certain had blossomed on his cheeks, he buried his head in her refrigerator and pretended to look for the beer. He grabbed a longneck bottle.

"Yes, um…well…" She cleared her throat. "The breakfast bar or the couch? Your choice."

"Is this like Angelo's, where I can pick inside or patio dining?" What was that kiss all about? He twisted the cap off his beer and tossed the top into her recycling bin. This was Ellie and they were hanging out. He wasn't supposed to be thinking about her exposed skin or those tiny freckles or how shiny her hair looked. Or how he wanted to keep on kissing her until she was breathless.

"Exactly like Angelo's…if you don't count the lack of fairy lights, table service or cannoli." She nodded her head several times. "Couch or kitchen?"

"Couch sounds okay. That's what I do at home." He picked up the box and she trailed behind with the plates and napkins. "And what's this no-cannoli business?"

She set the stuff on the coffee table and snapped her fingers. "Actually, I do have some. Let me take them out of the freezer so they can defrost while we eat the pizza."

He set the box down next to the plates. "Frozen cannoli?"

She huffed out a breath. "Really? You gonna be a cannoli snob, too?"

He lifted his hands up as if surrendering, the beer dangling from his fingers. "I'll allow it since you haven't had Mike's."

"Mike's?" She went back to the kitchen area and took the cannoli out of the freezer, setting the package on the counter with a *clunk*.

"It's a bakery in the North End of Boston and totally worth fighting wicked traffic to get there." He took a sip of beer and set the bottle down. "I'll bring you some real cannoli the next time I come back."

"Thanks, but in the meantime we'll have to make do with Trader Joe's." She came back and sat on the couch.

He lowered himself onto the cushion next to her, close but not enough to crowd her. Or to tempt him into doing something he might regret. But she'd been into that vestibule kiss, his inner voice reminded him.

She flipped open the cover on the pizza, filling the room with the scent of fresh dough and pepperoni. Grabbing a plate, she set a slice on it and handed it to him.

"And you said there wouldn't be any table service," he said as he folded the piece in half and took a bite.

"I haven't had a chance to talk to Craig, but I hear he was on cloud nine after his visit to the fire station. Thank you again for arranging it."

"Happy to do it." Especially since it had given him another excuse to hang out with Ellie. He set his plate down. "Almost forgot. Craig made me promise to show this to you."

He pulled his phone out of a pocket and thumbed through his pictures until he came to the one of the youngster fitted out in bunker gear and handed it to her.

"Will you look at that. How did you manage this?"

He shrugged, but he loved making her eyes shine like a freshly polished fire engine. "I remembered the guys talking about another house getting their hands on reasonably authentic bunker gear in miniature for a Make-A-Wish recipient. I contacted the firehouse that arranged it and they put me in touch with the people they'd used."

She leaned over and kissed his cheek. "Thank you."

"Sure. My pleasure. He seemed like a nice kid." Damn but he wanted to turn his head so his lips were on hers.

She took another slice and put it on her plate but left it on the low table in front of them.

"Where'd the remote go? I always keep it here on the

coffee table." She pointed to the exact spot where it had been until he'd picked it up.

"Were you referring to this?" He held up the remote, trying not to laugh at her expression.

She tried to grab it, but he managed to keep it out of reach. Her shirt pulled up when she lifted her arm, exposing her stomach. Once again, his body tightened at the sight. He did his best to temper his reaction. If he wasn't careful, she'd know *exactly* what she was doing to him.

"I just want to see what's on your watch list," he told her, pointing the remote and chuckling, hoping to cool his rioting hormones. "Let's see what we've got here. Wait a sec, what's all this sappy romance— Oomfff."

She'd blindsided him by making a dive for the remote, but he reacted by pulling it farther out of reach, and she landed across his lap and chest. She struggled to sit up but he put his arm around her, trapping her where she was. Her honey eyes darkened as he lowered his head. He felt her tense, but then she melted against him once his lips touched hers. Her lips tasted like cherry. He kissed his way across her jawline, nipped her earlobe and touched his tongue to the spot where her neck and shoulder met.

Suddenly, "Bohemian Rhapsody" began blaring from the kitchen.

He lifted his head. "What the…?"

"My phone," she said in a breathless tone.

He pulled away, feeling equal measures of relief and annoyance. What was he doing messing with Ellie? She was Meg's friend…*his* friend. *Way to screw up friendships, dumbass.*

The air in the room suddenly felt thick. It was hard

to breathe, as if the oxygen had been vacuumed out. The phone continued to blast the unmistakable tune.

He managed to suck in some air. "Going with a classic?"

That was so not what he'd wanted to say, but the things he wanted to say were probably best left unsaid.

"It's a classic for a reason," she shot back, using her hands and elbow to scramble off his lap. Thankfully that elbow missed his important bits.

He shifted and adjusted his jeans. *That was a close call...*

Ellie went into the kitchen, arguing with herself whether the interruption was a good thing. It wasn't as if she'd ever aspired to be a booty call. And he'd pulled back in a hurry, so maybe it had been a good thing that he'd gotten freaked out. She grabbed her phone and checked the caller ID. Craig's mom. Was she calling to thank her for introducing her son to Liam? Talk about irony.

Ellie listened to the woman on the other end, but her gaze and her attention was on Liam, whose attention was on the television. Had he, like her, gotten caught up in the moment?

After accepting the gratitude and telling her she'd pass that on to Liam, Ellie disconnected the call. She tugged on the hem of her T-shirt and went back into the living area.

"That was Craig's mom. She said she can't thank you enough for arranging everything for him. The kid-sized bunker gear was the icing on the cake. She said she's having trouble getting him to take it off." She picked up her plate and sank back against the cushions. "We should finish the pizza before it gets cold."

He cleared his throat and picked up the remote again. "I see you've got *Seinfeld* on your list. Wanna watch some of those episodes?"

"Sounds like a plan. Have—have you ever seen the show?"

"No, but I've heard a lot about it. Another classic for a reason?"

"Probably." Were they going to ignore what happened? "Do we need to…uh, talk about…"

When he frowned, she waved her hand back and forth between them.

He sat forward a little, resting his elbows on his knees. "Do *you* need to?"

She shrugged. Did she want to discuss it or ignore it?

He straightened up and touched her shoulder. "This wasn't a booty call, if that's what you're worried about."

Worried or hoping? She huffed out a laugh. "If it was, it would've been a first."

"C'mere." He pulled her next to him and draped an arm over her shoulder. "Let's see what this show is all about."

"Sounds like a plan." She smiled and snuggled against him. "Catching up on our pop culture knowledge. There's talk about Hennen's starting a trivia night."

"We'll be an unstoppable force."

She liked the way he used "we" so casually. Tonight might be eating pizza and cannoli while watching classic television, but she would cherish this time spent with Liam. It wasn't what they were doing but being together that mattered.

When the episode ended, he turned his head. "Is there a path to the lake?"

"Yes, and not only a nice path, there's a small gazebo with a swing. I sometimes go down there in the evenings to unwind. Letting nature surround me is calming."

He rubbed his chin. "Yeah, that's what I was thinking... a nice night to be surrounded by...uh, nature."

She bumped his shoulder. "You are so full of it."

"Is it working?" He wiggled his eyebrows.

She heaved a sigh, but she loved that the awkwardness after the kiss had dissolved. "Let me get my shoes on and grab a sweater."

"A sweater? Ellie, it's August."

"For your information, I don't have the same amount of body mass that you do to keep me warm and sometimes it gets cool down by the water...even in August."

"Then go bundle up." He tilted his head toward the mess on the coffee table. "I'll pick this stuff up and put the leftovers in the refrigerator."

"A sweater is not bundling up," she muttered as she scooted off the couch but turned back. "Thanks for cleaning up."

In the bedroom, she pulled on her sneakers and grabbed a cardigan sweater from her bureau drawer.

"Do you have your key?" He touched her arm as she started to pull the door shut.

"We're only going down to the lake."

"But it's—"

"Loon Lake," she interrupted.

He gave her a look. "Please tell me you don't do this when you're alone."

"I don't usually go alone to the lake after dark. I love

listening to the loons, but if I open my windows I can hear them from the safety of my bedroom since those windows face the lake."

Landscape lights lit the crushed shell path and the dog-day cicadas serenaded them from the surrounding trees.

"Meg loves listening to the loons at night as they settle in and call for their mates to join them," Ellie said as they made their way toward the water.

"Yeah, my mom was the same. She used to drag us kids down to the water's edge in the evenings."

Ellie reached for his hand and squeezed. "I know you both miss her."

When she would have pulled her hand away, he held on.

"Yeah, as a kid I grumbled when she insisted on boring stuff like walks to the lake to stand around and listen. She said we were making memories and that someday I would understand. I would give anything now to tell her I understand." He sighed. "I never told her."

"I don't think your mother expected you to thank her, Liam. She probably didn't thank hers, either. But she passed on that experience by giving you a happy, secure childhood. Just as you'll do for your kids."

"Pfft. I know I disappointed her by choosing the fire academy over college."

"I'm sure she wanted you happy in your career." Her heart went out to him, reacting to the sadness in his tone. How could he not know this?

When he made a disparaging sound, she stopped and turned toward him. Most of his face was in the shadows but she didn't need to see his expression to feel his skepticism. "It's true. She told my mom how proud she was of how much you helped with Meg and Fiona."

He shrugged. "It isn't hard to love Fiona."

"But you put your life on hold to help out so Meg could finish her degree." She longed to make him understand, wipe away the self-reproach she heard in his voice.

"Put my life on hold?" He huffed out a mirthless laugh. "All I did was move out of a sparsely furnished apartment to move back home. Not exactly a big sacrifice."

"You did it to help. That meant a lot."

"When Meg finally confessed about the pregnancy, my mom had it all worked out that she'd babysit while Meg finished college. But then Ma got sick and Meg was ready to drop out. I couldn't let that happen. Mom had already been disappointed when I joined the department before completing my degree."

"So why can't you believe how proud she was of you for doing that for your sister?" Her hand still in his, she tugged on his arm.

He sighed. "It's not so much believing as wishing I had done more for her."

"As someone who has had cancer, take it from me— it eased her mind about Meg and Fiona. That means a lot."

"Yeah?"

"Yeah."

They came to the small gazebo and sat side by side on the wooden swing that hung from the rafters of the ceiling. He still had her hand in his. Using his feet, he set the swing in motion.

"You have a sweet deal here. How did you find out about the apartment?" he asked.

"I was on duty when an estate agent passed through the ER. He heard me talking with some of the other nurses about trying to find a rental apartment. He gave me his card and said to call him. At first I thought it might be a scam but Meg and Riley came with me to check it out. Other than being a bit farther out of town than I'd like, it's perfect."

He glanced around. "It's quiet. Has the owner ever shown up?"

"Not yet. They were still doing the interior work on the main house when I moved in. So it honestly hasn't been completed for all that long."

"Have you been inside?"

"Before they finished up, some of the workmen let me take a tour."

"Do you think you'll stay here for a while?"

"For now, yeah. When I was growing up we lived next door to my cousins and I loved it. Especially as an only child, it was nice to have playmates. My cousins and I are still very close today. If I ever get married and have kids, I'd love to live close to family, let our kids grow up together." She left out the part of dreaming about living with him and a couple of kids next door to Meg.

Jeez, live in your head much? No wonder you don't have an active dating life.

"If?" He turned to look at her. "What's this 'if' business? You planning to dedicate yourself to your career?"

"No. I'd love to get married, but first someone has to ask me, and I'm still not convinced I'll be able to get pregnant." She hated to admit it, but that fact alone sometimes held her back. What if she met a nice guy who wanted kids and she wasn't able to give him that?

"Because of the cancer?"

"Because of the treatments but yeah...because of the cancer. The doctors say it's possible, but possible and probable are two different things."

"Then I hope it happens if that's what you want."

"I've learned not to dwell on things out of my control." She shrugged. "Besides, there's other ways. Since becoming friends with Mary, I've given a lot of thought to fostering or at least helping out with their summer camp once they get the cancer survivors part going."

"Yeah, that seems like a worthwhile project. Whoever thought that up must be a genius."

She laughed. "I thought so, too."

once, she didn't mind the interruption when she saw her caller was Liam.

"Sorry." Ellie pulled the phone from the front pocket of her purse. "Excuse me but I need to get this."

She had a pang of guilt but reminded herself that Colton had asked her for another woman's phone number. "Hey."

"Glad I caught you. Have you left the hospital yet?"

"No. Is there something wrong?"

"Nothing wrong. I simply hoped to catch you before you got all the way home. My dad and Doris arrived this afternoon and we're having an impromptu family cookout. Whaddaya say, Ellie, will you come?"

"But if it's family..." She was acutely aware of Colton watching her.

"You're family. Just say yes. You know you want to."

She clutched the phone tighter. Of course she wanted to say yes, but feared she was opening herself to more heartache. She glanced down at her scrubs. They were clean but they were still scrubs. "I'm not dressed for—"

"Did I mention it's a cookout?"

Could she pass up spending time with Liam? "Okay. What can I bring?"

"Just your cute self."

Colton's radio squawked and he held up his hands as if in surrender. "Gotta run. Catch you later."

Ellie waved as the EMT trotted away.

"Who's that with you?" Liam asked.

"Colton."

"The EMT?"

She nodded, then realized Liam couldn't see her. "Yeah, they brought in a patient as my shift was ending."

"So I'll see you in a bit?"

"I'm on my way."

Chapter Five

"Hey, Els, got any plans for tonight?"

The day after sharing pizza with Liam, Ellie had been on her way out of the hospital after her shift, but turned as Colton caught up to her. He and Mike had brought in a suspected heart attack just as her shift ended. Luckily, her replacement was already on duty for the night and she was able to leave.

She raised her brow. "Why? Did you lose the X-ray tech's phone number?"

"Aw, c'mon, you're not holding that against me, are you?" He stopped in front of her with a sheepish grin.

"No, but aren't you working?" she asked. Colton was a great-looking guy. One most women would be happy to date. But he had one big flaw. He wasn't Liam.

"My shift ends in an hour. Maybe we could—"

He was interrupted by "Bohemian Rhapsody." For

* * *

Liam pocketed his phone and walked across the yard to his sister's place. He glanced at his watch. How long would it take for Ellie to get here from the hospital? What if Colton distracted her? He stumbled over a small exposed root in Meg's yard.

Meg glanced up from putting condiments, utensils and plates on the picnic table. "Is Ellie coming?"

"Yeah. She was just leaving the hospital." He shoved his hands in his jeans.

Inviting Ellie had been Meg's idea. That's right. All Meg's idea. He had this thing with Ellie under control. Although she didn't say anything, Meg had a smug smile on her face.

Yeah, the joke was on her because he and Ellie were just hanging out, throwing her off the scent. "Got any cold beer, sis?"

Meg tilted her head toward the house. "In the refrigerator. Get me one while you're at it and don't shake it."

He rolled his eyes. "I'm not twelve."

She rolled her eyes right back at him. "No, you just act like it."

"Yeah, yeah. Keep it up and you can fetch your own beer."

"And you can get in your truck and drive to the store and get your own." She planted her hands on her hips.

A screen door banged shut.

Mac McBride stood on the porch, arms folded over his chest. "Exactly how old are you two?"

"She started it."

"He started it."

Doris emerged from the house and stopped beside Mac, who put his arm around her.

The looks they gave each other seemed to say broken hearts did mend. Liam shook his head at the thought. Avoiding all that pain in the first place sounded like a better course of action.

His dad's new wife—he had trouble thinking of Doris as a stepmother—had been a widow who'd lost both her husband and only child to a drunk driver. And yet she'd found happiness again with his dad, and showered Fiona and James with as much grandmotherly love as his own mother would have. For that, and for his sister's sake, he was glad his dad and Doris had taken another chance. Since Mac's retirement, they'd purchased a Class A motor home and spent months at a time traveling.

Doris handed James's baby monitor to Meg. "He's sound asleep. Since he had supper he may sleep through the night at this point."

"Thanks for helping." Meg hugged Doris.

"My pleasure. I need to finish my pasta salad. Want to help?" Doris turned to Mac.

"I'd love to help." Mac grinned. Turning to his kids, he scowled. "Can I count on you two to behave?"

"Tell him that."

"Tell her that."

Doris slipped her hand in Mac's. "Let's get while the getting is good."

After they'd gone into their motor home, which they had parked in the side yard, Meg set the baby monitor on the picnic table and sat down on the bench. "Whaddaya think? Don't come a-knockin' if this van's a-rockin'."

"Eww." Liam shuddered. That was one picture he didn't want in his head.

"You're welcome." Meg gave him a toothy grin. "Hey, I thought you were getting a beer."

"I—" He stopped as a Subaru pulled into the long driveway. "Ellie's here."

Instead of going into the house, he swerved and headed toward where Ellie was parking her car. Meg snorted a laugh and Liam slowed his steps. He was greeting a friend, that's all, like he might greet Nick Morretti, the engineer driver on his shift, or any one of the other guys. *And when was the last time you wanted to plant a kiss on Nick?*

He opened Ellie's car door. "Hey. Glad you could come."

"Thanks." She swung her legs out and stood.

Reaching down, he took Ellie's hand as she stepped out. He looked up in time to see Meg's smirk. Canting his head to one side, he crossed his eyes at her. Meg responded by sticking out her tongue.

"That your dad's?" Ellie pointed to the motor home parked off to the side.

"Yeah, that's Matilda."

"He named it?" She laughed. "I love it."

He could listen to that laugh for the rest of his life. He took a step back and cleared his throat. Where did that come from? They were hanging out while he was in Loon Lake. Friends. Period.

Meg wandered over. "Ellie, glad you could come. My brother was just getting us beers. Would you like one?"

He winked at Ellie. "Or how about some cheap wine?"

"Hey." Meg shook her head. "Have you no manners?"

Ellie laughed. "It's okay. It's an inside joke."

Liam frowned. *Inside joke.* Isn't that what couples shared?

Friends could share them, too, he assured himself.

* * *

Ellie turned around as tires crunched on the gravel. A county sheriff's vehicle drove up and parked behind her Subaru. She waved to Riley, who flashed the emergency vehicle lights in response.

"You didn't tell me the cops were hot on your tail." Liam draped an arm over her shoulder as they walked toward the picnic table. "You led them right to us."

Ellie grinned. "Hmm…maybe Riley came up with a few more felons for me to date."

"Am I ever going to live that down?" Meg groaned and walked past them, heading toward Riley.

"What have I missed here?" Liam demanded, his gaze bouncing between Ellie and Meg.

Meg turned back, shaking her head. "It's nothing. All a misunderstanding."

"Just before you showed up at the church luncheon, Meg was trying to fix me up with some guy Riley arrested," Ellie told him. "She seemed to think he'd make a great date for Mary's wedding."

Liam scowled. "What? Why would—"

"Like she said, a misunderstanding," Ellie said, and explained what they were talking about.

Riley had gotten out of the car and Meg threw her arms around his neck and kissed him.

"Guys. Could you save that, please? You have company." Liam waved his arms as if directing airliners to the gate.

Ellie shook her head. The man had no clue how fortunate he was to have a family so openly affectionate. Even her aunts, uncles and cousins were more subdued in her parents' company, perhaps because they remembered how much things had changed during the cancer treatments, especially when her future had been uncertain.

Riley glanced around. "Where is everyone? I was led to believe we were having a big family get-together."

Riley kept his arm around Meg's waist as they strolled over to stand next to the picnic table. Riley grabbed some chips out of the bag Meg had brought out earlier.

"James is napping after having a meltdown and your daughter has another—" Meg checked her watch "—five minutes of house arrest."

"Uh-oh." Riley grimaced. "Would I be wrong if I assumed those two things are related?"

"And now for the *Reader's Digest* version." Meg grabbed the last chip in Riley's hand. "Fiona yelled at James because he threw her brand-new Barbie into the toilet when she left the lid up. James lost his balance and fell on his butt, but I think the tears were because his beloved big sister was mad at him."

Riley winced as he reached into the bag for another handful of chips. "Please tell me he didn't flush."

"Thankfully, no. We sent in G.I. Joe to do a water rescue." Meg giggled and turned to Liam and Ellie. "See all the fun you guys are missing out on?"

Liam took a seat on the picnic bench. "I'm sure if Ellie and I were in charge, we'd have it all under control, sis."

Meg rolled her eyes. "You are so clueless, brother dear. Right, Ellie?"

Ellie smiled and nodded. What would it be like to be a permanent member of this affectionate family? She sat on the bench next to Liam. She had to keep reminding herself they were hanging out so Meg wouldn't continue her matchmaking.

"Hey, two against one." Liam gently squeezed Ellie's shoulder. "Riley, some help here."

"Don't look at me." Riley held his hands up in surrender and leaned over to kiss Meg again.

"Jeez, guys, please." Liam brought his open palm toward his face and turned his head.

Riley laughed, giving Meg a noisy, smacking kiss. "Where are Mac and Doris?"

"They're in the motor home. Preparing the pasta salad." Meg made air quotes as she said it.

Liam groaned and buried his head in his hands, his elbows on the picnic table. Riley snorted with laughter.

"What's so funny?" Ellie asked.

"Ever since catching his dad doing the morning-after walk of shame, Liam doesn't like thinking about what his dad and Doris might really be doing." Riley clapped Liam on his shoulder.

Liam lifted his head, giving Meg an accusing look. "You told him."

"Of course. He's my husband." Meg put her arm through Riley's.

"Well, no one's told me." Ellie tugged on Liam's arm.

Liam shot Meg a you're-so-gonna-pay-for-this look. "It was after I'd moved to my Dorchester place. Meg was still living with Dad and had asked to borrow something. I don't even remember now what she wanted—that's probably my attempt to block the whole incident from my memory. Anyway, I stopped by wicked early one morning before my shift to drop it off. I was in the kitchen when Dad was letting himself in the back door wearing the previous day's clothes and looking way too satisfied for my peace of mind."

Liam closed his eyes and shook his head. Ellie laughed, enjoying spending time with the McBrides and being reminded some families laughed and teased and loved openly. Her parents were still subdued, as if joking around and having fun was asking for trouble. They might not have always been as boisterous as some families, but enough that she missed the love and laughter when they disappeared.

Riley gave his shoulder a push. "Think of it this way, McBride—Mac's still got it at his age."

Liam looked appalled. "Why would I want to think about that?"

"Face it. We're gonna be that age someday." Riley leaned down and kissed Meg's forehead. "I need to change out of this uniform."

"Is Fiona allowed out of jail?" Riley asked on his way into the house.

"Yes, tell her she can come out but Mangy needs to stay in the house or he'll be pestering us while we eat."

"You left the dog with her?" Riley shook his head. "Not much of a punishment if she got to keep her dog with her."

Meg shrugged. "I felt bad about her new doll."

"Was it ruined?" Riley frowned.

"No, but now it's tainted. Forever destined to be Toilet Barbie."

Mac and Doris came out of the motor home and crossed the yard. Doris set a large covered Tupperware container on the picnic table.

"Ellie, I'm so glad you were able to join us," Doris said, and gave her a motherly hug.

Ellie returned the hug. "Thanks for including me."

"Of course, dear, why wouldn't we?"

Ellie caught Liam's frown in her peripheral vision. Had including her been Meg's doing? She needed to be careful, or she would find herself with a one-way ticket to Heartbreak Ridge.

Chapter Six

Ellie checked her watch. Liam would be arriving soon to pick her up for Brody and Mary's wedding. She'd spoken to him several times over the phone in the week since the family cookout, but they'd both been too busy working to get together. At least that was the excuse he'd used, and she'd accepted it.

A car door slammed and Ellie contorted herself into another unnatural position but still no luck. That damn zipper was unreachable, despite all her valiant efforts. Footsteps on the stairs signaled that Liam was getting closer. No getting around asking for his help. Sighing, she opened the door and stepped onto the landing.

Liam looked up and paused partway up the stairs, mouth open and feet on different steps. He wore a deep charcoal suit, white shirt and royal blue tie. She couldn't decide which was sexier—Liam in a suit and tie or

Liam in his red suspenders and turnout pants. *How about Liam in nothing at all?* a little voice asked, but she quickly pushed that away.

With all the excess saliva, Ellie had to swallow twice to keep from drooling. "Liam..." Was that breathless croak coming from her?

"Wow, look at you." He shook his head and continued up the stairs.

She'd splurged on a cream-colored dress with a scoop neck, gathered waist and sheer organza overlay from the waist down. The bright blue embroidered flowers on the dress made a bold statement, but the royal blue peep-toe platform high heels screamed *sexy*.

He came to a halt in front of her. "Are you sure we need to go to this wedding?"

"Why do you think I bought this dress and these shoes?"

"To impress me?" His tone was hopeful.

You better know it. "Ha! You wish. Come in."

"Oh, I wish for a lot of things. Want to hear some of them?" His mouth quirked up on one side.

"I'd love nothing better, but I don't want to be late for Mary's wedding." She did her best to keep her tone light and teasing as she stepped back inside. "However, I do need a favor from you."

Once they were inside her kitchen, she pulled her hair over her shoulder on one side and presented him with her back. "Can you zip this up the rest of the way?"

He made a noise that sounded like it was part groan, part growl.

She glanced over her shoulder. "Problem?"

He shook his head and swallowed, his Adam's apple

prominent. "I'm just not used to having wishes granted so quickly."

A low, pleasant hum warmed her blood. "Helping me zip up was on your list?"

He snapped his fingers and made a face. "That's right. You said 'up.' Every time you say 'up,' I hear 'down' in my head for some reason."

"And what is this? Opposite day?" Thinking about his easing her zipper down gave her sharp palpitations.

"A guy can hope." His fingers caressed the skin exposed by the gaping zipper.

She drew in her breath. Was she going to do this? "Of course, I will need help *after* the wedding."

His light blue eyes darkened and glinted. "Anytime you need help getting undressed I'm your man."

"Good to know." She cleared her throat. "Now could you zip me up? *U-P.* Up."

He complied and rearranged her hair, pressing a finger to a spot near her collarbone. "You have a freckle right there."

"I do?" She'd always disliked her freckles, but it didn't sound as if Liam felt the same.

She turned her head toward him as he leaned over her shoulder. He cupped her chin to angle her face closer and kissed her. The kiss was hot and yet sweet, full of unspoken promises, a combination that had her blinking back tears of happiness.

Though neither one mentioned the kiss during the ride to the church, Ellie couldn't help replaying it. After the simple wedding ceremony, they drove to the far end of the lake in Ellie's Subaru for the reception, so she wouldn't have to climb into his truck in her dress and heels.

"This place is gorgeous," Ellie remarked as she and Liam walked across the parking lot toward the covered outdoor pavilion overlooking the lake. Flickering chandeliers hung from the A-frame log ceiling, and the tables, draped in white cloths, had flower centerpieces surrounded by votive candles.

"Is this what you would call romantic?" Liam had his palm planted firmly on the small of her back as they entered the venue.

She laughed and looked up at him. "Yes. Brody said he wanted Mary to feel like a fairy princess on her wedding day."

He gave a low whistle. "You're telling me Brody planned all this?"

"What? You don't think guys can be romantic?" She enjoyed teasing him, especially when he took the bait. "That's like the ultimate aphrodisiac to a woman. She'll pick the romantic guy every time."

He scratched his scalp. "Huh…"

"Relax." She grinned. "Brody came to Meg and me, and we suggested trolling Pinterest for ideas and put him in touch with people who could make it happen."

"Who knew you could be such a tease?" His mouth crooked at the corner.

"It's the shoes." She angled her foot from one side to the other.

"Are they imbued with special powers?" His eyes glinted as he admired her heels.

"They must be because they're holding your interest."

"You've always held my interest, Ellie."

Ellie wanted to believe him, but thinking like that

was going to get her heart broken for sure. They were just joking around talking like that. Weren't they?

"Hey, wait up, you two," Meg called as she and Riley crossed the parking lot toward them.

Ellie let go of their conversation as they fell into step with the other couple and entered the wedding reception. During the meal, Ellie did her best to ignore Meg's calculating grin every time she looked at them.

When the music started, Liam held out his hand and invited her to dance. Having him hold her as they danced was even better than she imagined...and she'd done copious amounts of imagining over the years. Her current fantasies regarding Liam were very adult.

"What you said back at your place..." he began, and tightened his hold on her as they swayed to the music, "about needing help getting undressed..."

"Whoa." Even with the shoes he was taller and she had to look up to meet his gaze. "When did unzipping my dress turn into undressing me?"

He wiggled his eyebrows. "Huh, I guess my brain was connecting the dots."

"It was connecting something, all right," she said, but cuddled closer to him until they were barely moving.

"Ellie?" he whispered, his breath tickling her ear. "You need to know I'll only be here for another week, maybe less. Riley and I are almost finished with the reno."

"I always knew you weren't staying in Loon Lake." It hurt, but it was the truth and she'd accepted that.

"I wanted to be totally up-front about that."

"I'm a big girl. I'm not expecting this every time I get involved with someone." She waved her hand around at the wedding reception. And that was true, but she hadn't exactly been involved with a lot of guys. "Sometimes I just want to have fun."

Ellie couldn't help thinking dancing with Liam at the reception was like a prelude to what was coming next. After seeing the happy couple off to their honeymoon, she and Liam held hands as they walked to Ellie's car.

They didn't talk much on the way back to her place but the sexual tension was palpable—at least on her end. She threw a couple furtive glances at Liam, but his concentration seemed to be on driving. What if he didn't want this? She hated the thought of throwing herself at him if—

"Ellie?" He reached for her hand and enclosed it in his much larger one.

Oh, God. Was he going to tell her he changed his mind? Was he thinking of a way to let her—

"I hear you all the way over here."

"But I didn't say anything."

"But you were busy thinking it."

"Guilty," she admitted.

He angled a glance at her. "Are you having second thoughts?"

"Are you?"

"No, but I will respect your wishes."

"Then I'm wishing you'd drive a little faster. Pretend you're on your way to a fire."

"Fire?" He lifted an eyebrow. "More like a conflagration." Liam pulled the car into her driveway and glanced over at her as he parked the car. "Still with me?"

"Absolutely."

He took her hand as they climbed the stairs. Once inside her apartment, he kicked the door shut and took her into his arms. He brushed the hair off her cheeks with his thumbs. "Sweet, sweet Ellie, I'm praying you want this as much as I do."

More than you could ever imagine. "Yes."

He rained kisses along her jaw and neck; when he got to her collarbone, he paused.

"I've been thinking about these freckles all damn day," he said, and pressed his lips along her skin, followed by his tongue.

She shivered, and with a low growl he swept her up into his arms and carried her into the bedroom, where he pulled her dress up and over her head, dropping it to the floor at his feet. Laying her gently on the white comforter, he spread her hair around her head.

Easing over her, he caressed the exposed skin on her hip. "Look at what we have here."

She lifted her head. "My surgery scar?"

"Nope. More freckles, but these were hiding from me all this time," he said, and bent down to kiss above her hip.

Her nipples hardened as his hand neared her breasts, making her shiver. She sucked her breath in when his fingers found her breast and kneaded the flesh. He rubbed his palm over her hardened nipple through the lace.

Wanting more, wanting his mouth where his hand was, she arched her back to press closer to him.

He ran his fingertips along the top of her bra and sent shivers along her nerve endings. She pressed closer and he pushed the bra down, freeing her breasts.

"Finally," she moaned.

He chuckled. "Is that what you wanted?"

"I was ready to do it myself."

He made a tutting noise with his tongue. "I never knew you were so impatient."

"Only with you."

"Then maybe you'll like this," he said, and lowered his head and covered her nipple with his mouth. His tongue made twirling motions around the bud. At her sharp intake of breath, he began to suck gently. The moist heat of his mouth made her tremble with need.

When he lifted his mouth and blew lightly on the wet nipple, she nearly shattered right then and there. With clumsy fingers, she unbuttoned his shirt, needing to touch his bare skin.

He lifted his gaze to hers, his eyes glittering with something raw and primitive. Something she'd never seen in him before, and it thrilled her. She hadn't finished unbuttoning his shirt, but he simply pulled it over his head and tossed it on the floor. Standing up, he shed his pants and boxer briefs, then slowly lowered himself back down on the bed.

She pressed her lips against the warm, smooth skin on his chest; he tasted tart and salty.

His mouth brushed over hers in a light, caressing kiss that had her wanting to plead for more. He slid a hand under her nape and drew her closer.

She closed her eyes as his lips moved in gentle urgency over hers. Her blood felt like high-octane fuel racing through her body. Every thudding beat of her heart had her wanting him more and more, until her desire rose to a feverish pitch. She could feel a tension building within her in a push-pull sensation, leaving her hot and moist in a need for the full possession of her body by his.

His tongue demanded entry to her mouth and she

opened with a moan of pleasure as it danced with hers, cavorting back and forth, sliding and caressing.

His hand covered one of her breasts and sent shock waves down to her toes. With his other hand behind her he unclasped her bra and tugged it aside. Once again his mouth claimed her breast, his mouth sucking the nipple and teasing it with his teeth. Her other breast begged for the same attention and she ground her hips against him.

When his mouth touched the other nipple she thought she would explode from the pleasure and the longing. He gave that one the same attention, licking, sucking and nipping at the rigid nipple. As he lifted his mouth and blew on the nipple again, her hips twitched and bucked toward his erection.

All her nerve endings humming and sizzling, she reached up and twined her arms around his neck. She pulled him down, reveling in the way his weight felt on top of her. He kissed her with a searing hunger, as if he'd been waiting for her all his life. He feasted on her mouth like a starving man.

His mouth left hers and he trailed sweet, tantalizing kisses over her shoulders, stopping to kiss the freckles on her collarbone, then moved again to her breasts. He drew his tongue lightly across the underside of her breasts and toward her belly button. He kissed a spot on her hip and let his tongue drift over the elastic waist of her cream lace bikinis. She arched her hips up and buried her hands in his disheveled hair.

His breath flowing over her created goose bumps on her flesh and a mind-numbing sensation in her pleasure-fogged brain. Just when she felt she couldn't stand it a moment longer, he touched the spot that had been begging for attention and she exploded.

She'd barely come back to earth when a foil packet rustled and she reached up to take the condom, saying, "Let me."

He handed the packet to her, his eyes dark with desire and gleaming with anticipation.

His gaze locked on hers and held her in an erotic embrace before he thrust into her. He withdrew and thrust again, more deeply this time, all the while watching her, his blue eyes blazing with a light that should have blinded her. The depth of their connection shocked her, heated her from the inside out each time he filled her.

The need began to spiral to life within her for a second time and all thought was lost; she could only feel, drowning in sensation. He increased the pace as she tried to reach for her release. They both fell into the abyss at the same time, their heavy breathing the only sound in the room.

Liam climbed back into bed after taking care of the condom and pulled Ellie into his arms. He was still processing what they'd just shared. Somehow it transcended mere sex. That fact should scare him, but he was feeling too boneless and satisfied to worry.

She sighed and snuggled closer, resting her head on his chest. "That was…"

"Yeah, it was." He kissed the top of her head and rubbed his hand up and down her arm.

"I never knew freckles could be sexy." She caressed his chest.

He twined his fingers through hers. "You better believe it."

"I always hated them."

"And now?"

She giggled. "I guess they aren't so bad."

"What was the scar from?"

"Surgery."

"For the cancer?"

"Indirectly. They moved my ovaries aside to decrease the chances of becoming infertile due to the treatments."

"I guess the treatments can be as destructive in their own way as the cancer." He squeezed her hand. "So did the operation work?"

"I won't know until I start trying, but like I said, it's possible. Why?" She moved her head back to look at him.

Her silky hair brushing against his chest wasn't helping his current condition. "I don't have any more condoms with me."

"And I don't have— Oh, wait!" She sat up. "Would glow-in-the-dark ones work?"

What was his Ellie doing with glow-in-the-dark condoms? Was there even such a thing? "Ellie, what the…"

She grinned. "Leftovers from Mary's bridal shower."

He shook his head. "Do I even want to know?"

She leaned over and kissed him. "Probably not."

His body won out over his good sense. "Where are these condoms?"

She reached into the nightstand and held up a foil-wrapped strand.

He rolled his eyes. "Ellie, this better not ever become a topic of conversation at a future family gathering, like my dad's morning-after walk of shame."

"I wouldn't dream of it," she told him as they came together again.

* * *

Liam awoke with Ellie pressed against him, her back to his front, his arm around her waist as if he'd been afraid of her escaping while he slept. Where the heck had such a crazy thought come from?

Glow-in-the-dark condoms aside, he couldn't remember the last time—if ever—he'd been this affected. He tried to tell himself it was because they had become friends. It wasn't as if he had developed deeper feelings.

He and Ellie were hanging out while he was here and if that involved some sex, so be it. They were adults. They'd acted responsibly. Yeah, okay, the condoms had been unique but they'd used them. Responsible. He could go back to Boston, to his regular life, with memories of their jaw-dropping sex. He—

His phone began to buzz. Not wanting to wake Ellie, he slipped out of bed and found it in his pants. Going into the kitchen area, he answered the call from Chief Harris.

Several minutes later, he ended the call. He puffed up his cheeks and slowly released the trapped air.

"Who was that?"

He turned to face Ellie. She wore a very unsexy fleece robe but knowing she was probably naked underneath threatened to send his blood pooling below his waist. He did his best to shove those thoughts aside. Unlike Ellie, he hadn't stopped to put anything on before answering the phone.

"Liam?"

"It was my chief. Some of the guys are out sick and he was asking if I could cut my vacation a few days short. Guys are reaching their max for working extra shifts."

She huddled deeper into her robe. "So you need to go back today?"

"Yeah." He rubbed his chest at the sudden restricting tightness from the thought of leaving Ellie behind. Of Ellie becoming involved with someone like Colton. A guy who had the temerity to call her asking for another woman's phone number. Surely Ellie was smarter than that. "I need to jump in the shower and collect my stuff and let my sister know."

She smiled but it didn't reach her honey-gold eyes. "While you're in the shower, I'll make some breakfast."

He went to her and kissed her forehead. "Thanks. I—"

She waved her hand and stepped back. "We both knew it was temporary."

Chapter Seven

Finishing his twenty-four-hour shift, Liam checked his watch as he headed out of the redbrick firehouse located in a densely populated area of South Boston.

"Got a hot date waiting for you at home?" Nick Morretti, the driver engineer on Liam's shift, caught up to him.

"I have last night's episode of *Around the Horn* waiting for me on my DVR." Liam stopped and turned to hold the door open. He hadn't had a date in the two months he'd been home from Loon Lake. Two months since he'd last seen Ellie. Last held Ellie. It wasn't as if they'd broken up, because there was nothing to break. They'd had fantastic sex after the wedding; that's all. No regrets. No recriminations. It all sounded very civilized. So why did it feel so shabby? *We both knew it was temporary.*

"Thanks." Nick grabbed the door and followed Liam outside. "When you gonna take that plunge and settle down? You ain't gettin' any younger."

Liam shook his head. "Have you been talking to my sister?"

Nick laughed and fell into step beside Liam as they went into the early-morning October sunshine of the parking lot. "Don't want you missing out on all the good stuff that comes with marriage and kids."

"Face it, Morretti, you're just jealous because I get to go home and watch sports highlights in my undershorts." Yeah, the exciting life of a thirtysomething bachelor.

Nick laughed. "Is that what floats your boat these days, McBride?"

"It beats fishing a Barbie out of the toilet," he shot back. It did, didn't it?

Nick huffed out his breath. "Damn. When did Gina tell you about that?"

Liam barked out a laugh and tossed his gym bag into the bed of his pickup. "I was talking about my sister's kids, but do tell."

"And put you off marriage and kids? No way." Nick fished his keys out of his pocket. "Your sister, she's got what, two now?"

"And another on the way." Liam shook his head. "I swear all she and Riley have to do is look at each other and bam, I'm an uncle again. That's why I took all that vacation time up there in Vermont a couple months ago. I was helping Riley with an addition to their place. Only I didn't think they were going to need it quite this soon."

Nick opened the driver's door to a soccer mom–style SUV and climbed in. Sticking his head out the window, he wiggled his eyebrows. "And I suppose that attractive nurse I heard about was an entertaining perk."

Liam's fist tightened around his key fob and the truck's alarm beeped. Ellie wasn't a *perk*. She was… what? Some summer fun? Why did that have to sound so shabby? He wouldn't have thought that with anyone else.

He lifted his chin to acknowledge Nick's departing wave and climbed into his truck. He was bushed from taking extra shifts at a part-time station, but working had helped keep his mind off Ellie. That's the explanation he was going with. A decent few days of uninterrupted sleep and he'd be back to his old self, stop wondering what Ellie was doing. And he'd stop thinking about her honey-gold eyes, the way her hair smelled like flowers he didn't know the name of, and stop tasting the cherry flavor of her lip gloss on his tongue. Yeah, sports highlights, breakfast and stop mooning over Ellie sounded like a workable plan.

Ellie drew her knees up to her chest and bounced her feet on the concrete stoop of Liam's three-decker in the Dorchester section of Boston. A perfect example of the city's iconic multifamily housing units, the colorful home towered above her, looking like three small homes neatly stacked one on top of the other. The large bay windows curving around the right side of the building reminded her of a castle turret. No moat, but the roots from the lone tree in front of Liam's house had cracked and lifted the sidewalk as if trying to escape its concrete jungle. Poor tree.

God, first a car commercial last night and now a stupid tree. She swiped at a useless tear with the back of her hand. Damn her hormones for running amok and turning her into a crier. If this kept up much longer, she'd have to learn better coping skills. Not to mention perfecting those before Liam arrived home.

She inhaled and stretched her neck to glance up and down the quiet street. Why hadn't she called or texted first? Just because he was completing a twenty-four-hour shift this morning didn't mean he'd come straight home. He might stop off somewhere to eat or... She hugged her knees tighter. Or he might be with another woman at her place. She closed her eyes and swallowed against a fresh wave of nausea. What if he was bringing a woman home? After all, it had been eight weeks since their— Her chest tightened painfully as she searched for the right word to describe what they'd had. What had it been? A fling? An affair? Friendship with benefits?

Sighing deeply, she turned her head toward the glossy chestnut-stained front door behind her. What if there was a woman in there right now also waiting for Liam to come home? She made a choking sound before turning to face the street again.

No, there couldn't be, because if *she* saw a strange woman on her front porch for thirty minutes, she'd open the door and demand to know what was going on. However, it would serve her right for not calling ahead if there was another woman. She'd have to laugh it off and say something like, "I was in the neighborhood and..."

"Yeah, like he's gonna buy that," she muttered. Heck, Meg hadn't believed her lame excuse when Ellie had asked about Liam's work schedule. Curiosity had been evident in Meg's expression, but for once she didn't meddle. Not that it mattered, because Ellie wouldn't be able to hold Loon Lake gossip off for very much longer.

She could tell the people she worked with were already getting suspicious by the looks they gave her.

She sighed and rested her forehead on her knees. Short of abandoning her family, friends, job, future plans and everything she held dear in Loon Lake, swallowing her pride to confront Liam was inevitable. Of course, showing up with no prior notice might not be the best way to begin this particular conversation. Lately her head had been elsewhere, but she needed to do this in person. This wasn't something that could be handled in a text or even a phone call.

The low rumble of a truck engine alerted her and she sat up and braced her shoulders as a late-model gray pickup turned onto the street and slowed. *Liam.* And he was alone. Thanking whatever lucky stars she had left, she stood and shook her legs to straighten her jeans.

Liam maneuvered his truck into a parallel spot two houses away. She swallowed hard as he shut off the engine. The door slammed shut.

"Here goes nothing," she whispered, and stepped away from the front stoop.

He walked around the back of the truck and she drank in all six feet two inches. Still dressed in his uniform of navy blue pants and matching shirt with the red and bright yellow Boston Fire Department patch, he looked as though he'd just stepped off a beefcake charity calendar. The only things missing were his turnout pants with those sexy red suspenders. Her mouth watered at that seductive image. At least something other than nausea was making her mouth—

"Ellie?"

"It's me," she said with forced brightness and a fake smile.

He frowned. "Is something wrong? Meg, the kids… or you? You haven't—"

"No. No." She waved her hands in quick, jerky movements. *Scare the poor man, why don't you?* Yeah, she should've warned him of her visit but what would she have said if he'd asked why she was coming? For all she knew, he'd moved on from this summer. Unlike her. "Everyone is fine. Sorry. I should have called ahead but…"

He lifted his arms and embraced her in a welcoming hug. She threw her arms around him, gathering strength from his solid warmth. Wait…was he sniffing her hair? His arms dropped away before she could decide and she let go, despite the desire to hold tight. No clinging. She was an adult and could take care of herself. This trip was to deliver news. That's all.

She glanced back at the front door. No outraged woman bursting out demanding an explanation. One less thing to fret about. A small victory but she'd take it. "I, uh… I hope I'm not interrupting anything."

He draped an arm over her shoulder, gave her a quick shoulder hug and let go. "Nah, I just got off work."

"I know. I mean… I checked with Meg before I came." She scuffed the toe of one red Converse sneaker against the concrete. Doing this on his front porch was not an option. She sighed and motioned with her head toward the house. "You gonna invite me in, McBride?"

He pulled out his cell phone. "Sure, Harding, just let me tell the Playboy bunnies inside to exit through the back."

She rolled her eyes. "Yeah, right. Getting them to hide your porn stash is more like it."

"Ouch." He pocketed his phone with a devastating

grin, then motioned for her to go onto the porch ahead of him.

"I won't take up too much of your time." *Just long enough to change your whole life.*

On the porch, she stood to the side so he could unlock the door. He smelled faintly of garlic and tomato sauce. "You on kitchen duty?"

"Why? Do I smell like an Italian restaurant?" He lifted his arm, sniffed his sleeve and laughed, his eyes crinkling in the corners, the wide grin deepening those adorable grooves on either side of his mouth.

Ellie's toes curled. Score one for her newly heightened sense of smell. Except she didn't need to go where his sexy laugh and her rioting hormones wanted to take her. This trip wasn't about that. And once she told him why she'd come, he wouldn't be interested, either. "You never did bring me any cannoli from that Italian bakery you told me about."

"Mike's?" His light blue eyes flashed with mischief. "Sorry, Harding, but even if I'd gotten some, believe me, they would not have made it all the way to Vermont in the same truck as me."

God, but she'd missed him. She was such a sucker for that teasing glint in his eyes, but nevertheless she made a disparaging noise with her tongue. "McBride, it's a three-hour drive."

"Exactly," he said with a firm nod and a wink. "Sorry, but you'll have to make do with frozen."

She gave him a playful shoulder punch before following him into the inner hallway. A stairway led to the upper units on the left and the entrance to the ground floor unit was on the right. Liam unlocked his door and pushed it open, lifting his arm so she could scoot under.

No sexy heels today to add an extra three inches to her five feet three inches.

Flooded with morning sunlight from the large bay windows, the living room was standard, no-frills bachelor fare, with a brown distressed leather couch and matching recliner facing a giant flat-screen television with an elaborate sound system. Two empty beer bottles, a pizza box and wadded-up napkins littered the coffee table along with an array of remote controls. A sneaker peeked out from under the couch. The sunny room, even the clutter, was like a comforting arm around her shoulder and it warmed her. She could do this.

He cleared his throat. "Sorry about the mess."

"It's a wonderful space. I love these windows. They give you so much natural light." She set her purse on the couch.

"Thanks. Meg says if I had some taste, this place could be great." He tossed his keys on the coffee table and glanced around. "She calls my decorating style the 'under arrest' method…everything lined up against the walls as if waiting to be frisked and handcuffed."

Ellie laughed, picturing Meg chastising him. "Sisters."

A new and unfamiliar awkwardness rushed in to fill the silence. Had sex messed with their friendship? Had he moved on? It was not like they'd made any promises to each other or anything. Ellie rubbed the pad of her thumb over her fingers and swallowed another, more urgent, wave of nausea.

"I guess you're—"

"Would you like—"

Bitterness coated her tongue, making it curl in warning. If she didn't get to a bathroom—stat—she was going to throw up all over Liam's glossy wood floor. She covered her mouth with her hand, barely managing to gag the word, "Bathroom?"

His brow furrowed as he turned and pointed. "Down the hall. First door on the left."

She stumbled into the bathroom, slammed the door and dropped to her knees in front of the toilet. Hugging the bowl, she threw up the breakfast she'd convinced herself to eat before driving to Boston. Yuck. It would be a long time before she could eat oatmeal again…if ever.

Well, there was one bright spot to this whole debacle. At least he hadn't had a woman with him.

Pacing the hall outside the bathroom, Liam calculated ambulance response times against how quickly he could drive her to Brigham and Women's Hospital in midmorning traffic. Listening to Ellie being sick brought back memories of his ma spending hours puking in the bathroom after endless rounds of chemo. The word *cancer* blocked his field of vision like flashing neon. No, that was silly, Ellie had been in perfect health eight weeks ago. God forbid, but what if she was in Boston for an appointment at the Dana-Farber Cancer Institute? No, Meg would have said—

He flung the door open with such force it banged against the wall and bounced back, hitting his arm.

Ellie sat hunched over the bowl and he knelt down beside her. "My God, Ellie, what's wrong? Should I call paramedics? Or I could—"

She held up her hand and croaked out, "No," before the retching began again.

He pulled her hair away from the porcelain with one

hand and rubbed her back with the other. Things he could've—should've—done for his ma but hadn't because he was busy burying his head in the sand, convinced she would beat the cancer. His chest tightened, but with the ease born of practice, he shoved unwelcome emotions aside. He refused to fall apart. If he could run into a smoke-choked inferno, he could handle this. Right? "Tell me what's wrong."

She flushed the toilet, sat back and wiped her mouth with the back of her hand.

He reached up and grabbed a towel off the sink. "Here."

"Thanks." She wiped her mouth and hands before giving the towel back. "I'm okay now."

A chill ran through him and he searched her face as if he would find an answer there. "Are you sure?"

She nodded vigorously and began to rise. He tossed the towel aside, put his hand under her elbow and helped her up.

"May I?" She motioned toward the sink.

He sidestepped to give her a little more room to maneuver, but she was pale and sweating so he was going to be a jerk and stay close, even if he had to crowd her personal space. He didn't want her passing out on him. She turned on the faucet, captured water in her cupped hand and rinsed her mouth. He leaned past her for the discarded towel and mentally kicked himself for not going to Vermont to visit her. Why had he fought his own instincts to call or text her on a daily basis? Yeah, that wouldn't have made him look needy or anything.

She splashed water on her face and he handed her the towel. After she dried her face, he offered his bottle of mouthwash. She glanced from the uncapped plastic bottle in his hand and back to him, a frown creasing her brow.

He shrugged. "What? I lost the cap. Swig it."

"You're such a guy," she muttered.

"And I'm sure you meant that in the kindest possible way." He grinned, relaxing because the bantering was familiar, comfortable, easy to handle. That was his Ellie and— Wait. What was this "his Ellie" stuff about?

She rolled her eyes but raised the bottle to her lips.

Folding his arms across his chest, he watched while she rinsed her mouth and spit into the sink. Now that her skin had lost its previous pallor, she looked more like the Ellie he'd left in Vermont, the healthy one. His friend. The one he just happened to—

He shifted his stance and turned his thoughts away from Ellie's eyes and upturned nose with the light smattering of freckles. He'd put himself back out there in the dating world soon and life would return to normal. That's what he wanted, wasn't it?

"Do you mind?" She bumped him with her hip. "A little privacy, please."

She also had freckles on that hip. *What are you doing?* Thinking about Ellie's skin was not the first step in getting back to normal. "Can I get you something to eat?"

Those honey eyes widened. "Really? You're talking food after my little display?"

Damn she was right, but he needed something to do. Standing around feeling helpless was not something he enjoyed. He needed to be productive. "Hmph, coffee then."

She shuddered.

What the heck? Ellie loved her morning coffee. Now

she was scaring him. "Since when don't you like coffee?"

She glared at him. "Oh, I don't know, maybe since I just threw up what I had this morning."

Yeah, that was a lame question, but he hated not knowing what was wrong. "Fair enough. What would you like?"

"Got any decaf tea?"

Unfolding his arms, he stepped away. "I think I still have some from…"

"From who?"

"From Meg. The last time she was here she wanted decaf, so she bought a box." He frowned at her sharp tone. From the moment he'd seen her sitting on his front steps, she'd thrown him off-balance. "What, Ellie, do you think there's a woman in the closet waiting for you to leave?"

Her eyes narrowed but she didn't say anything. He ground his teeth. Damn, why couldn't he just keep his big mouth shut? Because she was hiding something from him. He just knew it and he didn't like it. Nor did he like the way he wanted to pull her into his embrace, bury his face in her soft hair and let her sweetness take his mind off the restlessness that had plagued him these past two months.

He sighed into the strained silence, regretting his remark. Maybe if he had visited her since their time in Loon Lake, he'd know what was going on with her and there wouldn't be this weird vibe between them. "I'll go check and see if I have any tea bags."

"Thanks. I'll be out in a minute." She shut the door behind him with a soft *snick*.

He found the tea in a cupboard and put some water on

to heat. While he waited for the water to boil, he stuck a pod in his coffee maker. Sleep was probably out of the question so he might as well enjoy some caffeine. Why she had come was a mystery, but something told him Ellie wasn't there to renew their friends-with-benefits arrangement. A morning filled with fantastic sex was looking less and less likely.

Ellie appeared in the doorway as he poured boiling water into a mug with her tea bag. As always when he saw her, his heartbeat sped up. It would appear her red sneakers had a similar effect on his libido as those sexy bright blue heels from the wedding. Like that wasn't messed up or anything.

His gaze rose to her face to take in the pink nose and shiny eyes. His stomach tumbled. Oh, Christ, had his tough-as-nails ER nurse Ellie been crying? Had he caused that with his thoughtless comment? What the hell was wrong with him saying stupid stuff like that, to Ellie of all people? She was the last person he wanted to hurt with a careless remark.

"Your tea." He handed her the hot mug, but what he really wanted was to shake her and demand she tell him what was going on. Or to grab her close and never let her go. Keep her safe forever. But keeping her safe was impossible because cancer didn't respect how much or how many people cared.

She wrapped her hands around the chipped ceramic as if warming them. "Thanks."

"I'm…uh…" What was wrong with *him*? This was Ellie and they'd talked endlessly for hours when they weren't—*hey, remember, we're not going there.* "I hope you like that kind. Meg bought it."

"This is fine." She jiggled the bag up and down. "Got any milk?"

"Let me check." He pulled the milk out of the refrigerator and sniffed the open carton. "Yeah, I do."

Her sudden laughter sent a tingle along his spine. He'd missed that laugh, her unique view of the world, her friendship. Okay, that's what was wrong with him. Ellie hadn't been just a sexual partner like others but a true friend. Relieved to find a reasonable explanation for the way he'd been feeling, he grinned. "We can go in the living room and sit."

"Yeah, that furniture looks more...comfortable."

His gaze landed on the wicked ugly collapsible card table and metal folding chairs from his dad's basement that doubled as a dining set. Not that he ever once dined on it. Eating takeout in front of the TV was more his style. Cooking for the guys while on shift was different from preparing something just for himself. "I haven't gotten around to doing much in here yet."

Her golden eyes sparkled. "Why? Did the couch or recliner resist arrest?"

"Took me a while to read them their rights." His mood was buoyed by the shared moment. Yeah, he'd missed that wacky humor of hers.

"You should get Meg to help with the decorating." She dropped her used tea bag into the wastebasket in the corner. "She's done a fantastic job with her kitchen and the new addition. The entire place really."

"I think she's got her hands full at the moment with being pregnant again. They didn't waste much time after James was born." He was happy for his sister, but seeing Meg so settled had him looking more closely at his own situation. And he didn't always like what he saw. But that was crazy, because as he'd told Nick, he was doing exactly what he pleased. He had a full life.

Ellie clucked her tongue. "She's happier than I've ever seen her. I hope you didn't say anything stupid like that to her face."

He picked up his coffee and followed her into the living room. "It wouldn't do any good if I did. As she's been telling me since she was five I'm not the boss of her."

"No, but she respects your opinion." She sat back on the couch but scooted forward when her feet dangled above the floor. "Besides, you like Riley."

He plopped down in the recliner. "I do as long as I don't have to think about what he and my sister get up to."

"Or your dad and Doris?"

He groaned and shook his head. "At least they're not popping out kids as proof."

She took a sip of her tea and set it on the table next to the couch. The sunshine streaming in through his uncovered windows made the highlights in her shiny hair glow, and he itched to run his fingers through all those dark and reddish strands. He tried to think of a word to describe it and couldn't. *Brown* was too plain a term to describe all that lustrous silk.

"What color is your hair?" Oh, man, had he actually asked that out loud? What was wrong with him?

"What?" She gave him a quizzical look.

He shrugged and hoped his face wasn't as flushed as it felt. "Meg has a thing about people calling her hair red and I, uh, just wondered if you had a name for your color like she does."

She ran a hand over her hair. "It's chestnut. Why?"

He nodded, but didn't answer her question. He'd embarrassed himself enough for one day. "Are you planning on telling me why you're here?"

She rubbed her hands on her thighs and drew in a deep breath. "I know we decided this summer was no strings attached, but—"

"About that, Ellie, I—"

"I'm pregnant."

Chapter Eight

Ellie winced. She hadn't meant to blurt it out like that, but he'd been acting strangely. Not that she could blame him, considering her showing up unannounced and then madly dashing to the bathroom. She could imagine him thinking the worst but that question about her hair color... What was that about? She shifted in her seat and glanced over at him. "Liam?"

He stared at her, his eyes wide, his mouth open, his breathing shallow. She'd imagined all sorts of scenarios during the drive to Boston, including him being stunned and angry, surprised and excited. The latter one was the one she preferred but not the most reasonable. *You left out the one where he declares his undying love and proposes.* Yeah, pregnancy hormones might be messing with her, but she was still tethered to reality. She'd been flummoxed to learn she was pregnant. Imagine poor Liam.

At least she knew now the cancer treatments hadn't rendered her sterile. Of course this wasn't the way she would've planned starting her family. Did wanting to be happily married first make her a prude?

"Are you going to say anything?" she asked, unable to stand the silence a moment longer.

He sprang from his chair as if galvanized by the sound of her voice, and came to sit next to her on the couch, crowding her space. He took her hand in his and rubbed his free one over his face. "Are you sure? Did you take a test? See a doctor?"

She tilted her head, lowered her chin and gave him the *are you kidding me* look. "Hello? Nurse Ellie here."

"Oh. Right." He closed his eyes and pinched the bridge of his nose. "This is… I mean… We… I… You…"

"Yeah, we did, but nothing is one hundred percent. Not even glow-in-the-dark condoms." Maybe Liam was as fertile as his sister. Of course now might not be the best time to point out that observation. Maybe someday they'd be able to get a chuckle or two out of it.

"Have you been to a doctor yet?" he asked.

"Not yet. I wanted to tell you before I went. In case you wanted to…to be involved…" Her voice trailed off.

Then she drew in a breath and plunged in with her prepared speech. "Look, I get that this is a lot to take in, but I want you to know I'm not going to force you to do anything you don't want. I have a good job and a great support system with family and friends in Loon Lake and—"

"Have you told anyone yet?"

"What? Why? Tell me why you would ask me something like…like… Liam?" Her voice had risen with each word; blood rushed in her ears.

He lifted their entwined hands and pressed them close to his chest. "Christ, Ellie, don't look at me like that. I figure you must've already come to a decision or you wouldn't even be here now telling me about the baby." He pulled her closer so she was practically on his lap. "Besides, you know me better than that. I know the ability to have children has been a concern of yours, and knowing how much you love kids, I'm sure you want them."

Relief washed through her and she nodded against his chest, the faint garlic aroma making her empty stomach rumble. Really? Food at a time like this? *You'd rather be thinking about sex?* "So why did you ask if I'd told anyone?"

He rubbed his thumb over her palm. "I was there when it happened, so I should be there when you tell your parents. At least I assume you're planning to tell them."

For the first time since coming to Boston, she was able to take a deep breath and released it with a laugh. Relief, or maybe it was oxygen, making her giddy. "I know it's early to be telling people but what happened in your bathroom is only a part of what's been happening. I either avoid my family for another month or tell them why I'm so tired, dizzy and pale. I don't want my mom thinking the cancer has returned. And it's not something I will be able to hide for very long from my family."

"You'd be surprised. I remember Meg hid it for as long as she could." He squeezed her shoulder.

"Your sister's situation was different. Meg was nineteen, still living at home, and Riley had left town, possibly forever. I'm twenty-seven, employed and, if that's not enough, I happen to know where you live." Why in heaven's name was she arguing with him? She should be ecstatic and yet she was…what? Disappointed because he hadn't pledged his love? This was Liam. Over the summer he had become not just a lover but also a friend. Still, he wasn't the most emotionally available guy she knew. Supportive was good. Supportive worked.

"I don't know about your parents, but my dad has this tone of voice…" He leaned against the couch cushions, drawing her back with him. "Makes me feel twelve all over again when he uses it."

"My mom…she gets this look." She blinked. Damn, but she'd never been a crier. She was smart, practical Ellie, a cancer survivor. A survivor who decided she wanted a fling with the deliciously sexy fireman who also happened to be a friend. She'd wanted to experience something a little wild, maybe even a little wicked. Of course she should have known better than to fall for her temporary fling. "I guess I'm a total failure at this fling business. Not getting pregnant must be like, what, number one on the no-no list?"

"A rookie mistake." He brushed his knuckles across her back.

She blew the hair off her forehead. "A big one."

He gently tucked those stray hairs behind her ear. "I'm sure your dad will be more likely to lay the blame on me."

She sat up straighter and pulled away so she could look at him. "I'll talk to my dad, make him understand that forcing someone into ma—into something they don't want isn't a solution."

He untangled himself and stood up, looking at her with that little half grin. "Wanna explain that to Mac, too?"

"I'm sure your dad will be fine." She huffed out a mirthless laugh. "He dotes on Fiona and James. He loves being Grampa Mac. And he has to know at your age that you're, uh, sexually active."

"Did you want to tell Mac while I'm here in Boston?"

"My dad and Doris are on another one of their jaunts in their motor home and not due back until next week." He stopped pacing and perched his butt against the windowsill. "I do need to tell Meg. If she finds out before I tell her, she'll never let me hear the end of it. What about you?"

"I'll tell my parents and since we'll be telling Meg, I'd like to tell Mary before she hears it from someone else. We've become good friends since she's moved to town. I can call her or stop by the farm."

Liam chuckled. "Meg likes to complain about Loon Lake gossip reaching me down here, but she's usually the one to call and tell me stuff. She claims that she's doing it before the chatter reaches me."

"You can still change your mind about coming with me to talk to my parents." She was giving him an out but prayed he wouldn't take it.

"No, I want them to know I'm not some random guy that got you—"

"Gee, McBride, thanks a lot." She wasn't about to confess to Liam how few guys she'd been intimate with… ever. And this wasn't how she'd imagined she'd feel when having a baby. Instead of celebrating with the man she loved, this was beginning to feel more like triage. She scooted off the sofa to go and stand in front of him.

"What? I only meant—"

"I know what you meant." She sighed but couldn't help leaning into his warmth. "That's the problem."

"I know you don't sleep around. What I'm saying is I need to face your dad. Apologize and—"

Her gaze clashed with his. "Liam? Zip it."

"Right."

"So, we need to break the news to my parents and Meg. Is…" She cleared her throat and took a step back, needing space before asking this next question. Correction, she needed space before receiving his answer. "Is there anyone else you might need to tell?"

"Like? Oh, you mean…" He straightened up and away from the windowsill and took a step, closing the distance she'd put between them. "There hasn't been another woman since…there's no other woman."

She released the breath she'd been holding. That tidbit warmed her more than she would've imagined. "Me, either."

"That's because I'm irreplaceable." He flashed her one of his devilish, intensely sexy smiles.

She gave him a backhanded slap on the arm, but she couldn't wipe the silly grin off her face. Or the relief from her heart.

Liam scrubbed his scalp vigorously as he lathered the shampoo and tried not to think, but Ellie's *I'm pregnant* was stuck on an endless loop in his head. No question he needed to step up and be there for Ellie and their child. He ducked his head under the shower spray and rinsed. Ellie would be a great mom. Exhibit one: she wasn't hiding in the bathroom using taking a quick shower as an excuse to build up much-needed defenses.

On a scale from an unplanned pregnancy to Ellie's cancer returning, the pregnancy was less scary every time, but that didn't mean he wasn't scared. Being a dad had been a nebulous idea for the future. Not on today's to-do list.

When he'd seen Ellie waiting for him on his steps, it had taken all his willpower to remain casual, to not confess how much he'd missed her, to not tell her how many times he'd thought about her. The hug he'd given her had been meant as platonic, two friends greeting each other, but the moment she'd been in his arms, he'd wanted her with an intense ache. And it hadn't been all physical. He could handle simple lust but this felt like more. More than he wanted to admit or accept.

Angry with himself for dwelling, he snapped the faucet off, grimacing when the building's ancient pipes rattled and groaned at his careless treatment. He stepped out of the shower, snatched a towel from the rack and dried off, dressing in jeans and a long-sleeve pullover shirt.

He grabbed a pair of socks and went back in his living room, where he found Ellie seated on the couch, watching television and looking relaxed. But the trash was gone from the coffee table, the remotes were lined up like soldiers, except for the one in her hand, and both of his sneakers sat by his recliner. Yeah, Ellie liked organization and structure.

"You didn't have to clean." He scooped up his sneakers and sank into the chair.

"I'd hardly call throwing a pizza box away cleaning." She waved her free hand in a dismissive gesture, but she was white-knuckling the remote in the other.

Before he could think of something to say, she prattled on. "Did you know that there's a nonprofit organization that studies and ranks tall buildings? Evidently they give out awards or something. Who would have thought to give awards to skyscrapers?"

She continued her one-sided discussion while he pulled the socks on.

"Isn't that interesting?" She peered at him, an expectant expression on her beautiful face.

"Uh-huh." He stuffed his feet into his beat-up running shoes, all the while trying to figure out where she was going with all this skyscraper talk.

She thrust out her lower lip. "You're not even listening."

He met her accusing glare and tried not to smile at her being indignant on behalf of inanimate objects. He longed to take that plump lower lip between his teeth and nip it so he could then soothe it with his tongue and then— Whoa. What happened to not going there?

"Liam?"

"I'm listening…honest…nonprofit…tall buildings… awards. See? But I fail to understand why you're sounding like the Discovery Channel all of a sudden." Where was all this going? Had he missed something?

"Would you prefer I sit here and cry?" She set the remote on the table and sniffed.

"God, no. Tell me more about these awards. They sound fascinating." He crowded beside her on the couch. When he put his arm around her, she leaned into his side and he rested his cheek on her hair. Her chestnut hair. Now he needed the name of the flowers it smelled like, but he damn sure wasn't going to ask her—at least not today. Her subtle scent surrounded him like whirling smoke. "I told you, I'm not going anywhere and I'm gainfully employed. That has to count for something."

She sniffed. "But you only wanted a short fling."

He tightened his embrace. Ellie would demand, and deserved, more than what he could give to this relationship, but he had to try if they were going to be parents. "But we're friends. We'll be friends having a baby."

"Have you forgotten you live here in Boston, and I live in Vermont?" She sighed, a sound filled with frustration.

Ellie wasn't a quitter and neither was he. It would take some adjusting, but they could work this out. "Now that you've mentioned it, there's plenty of room in—"

She pulled away. "Forget it. I'm not moving in with you."

Huh, that stung. Way more than he would've thought. And definitely more than he liked. Especially since that wasn't what he'd been suggesting. "I wasn't asking. My second-floor tenant is—"

"No, thanks. I wouldn't like the commute to work or the high city rents." She shot him a sour look.

"I haven't said anything about charging you rent."

"And I don't want to be responsible for putting you in a financial bind. Don't you need both rents to make the mortgage?"

Yeah, losing a rent would make it tough, but he wasn't about to admit that to her. "You let me worry about that."

How were they supposed to work things out if she kept throwing up roadblocks? He tried to pull her back against him, but she resisted. Was she upset because he hadn't asked her to move in with him? "In case you hadn't noticed, Boston has hospitals."

"Why do I have to be the one to move?" she sputtered. "Vermont has fire departments."

In Vermont, he wasn't in line for a promotion. In Vermont, he wasn't a fourth-generation firefighter. Loon Lake was a part-time house. He needed full time with benefits.

And the smaller the battalion, the longer it took to rise in the ranks. "They're not the Boston Fire Department."

"Oh, excuse me." She scowled. "Vermont might not have the honor of having the first fire department in the nation, but they know how to fight fires in Vermont. Last I heard they'd traded in their horses for shiny red trucks."

"I'm a fourth-generation Boston firefighter. It's a tradition that might continue with…" He glanced at her still-flat stomach. Would there be a fifth generation?

She placed a hand over her abdomen as if protecting it from him. "And maybe she won't want to be a firefighter."

"She?" All thoughts of their argument flew out of his head. He swallowed hard. How could a simple pronoun make his stomach cramp? "You already know it's a girl?"

"No, but I couldn't continue to say 'it,' so I started saying she. I figure I have a fifty-fifty shot at being right." She leaned back against the cushions, her expression smug.

"I see." By next year at this time, there'd be a new little person in his life, one he'd be responsible for and— He pushed those thoughts aside. One problem at a time. "So, you'll think about moving here?"

"Nope," she said.

Argh. Why was she being so stubborn? That would be the perfect solution. *You mean perfect for you.* He blocked out the accusing voice in his head. "Why not? Your skills would transfer to any of the emergency rooms here and you could probably earn more, too."

"But I wouldn't be happy. I like living in Loon Lake.

I like where I am, the people I work with." She crossed her arms over her chest.

"But didn't you say you were looking for a new job?" He seized on what he could to convince her while trying to ignore the way her crossed arms pushed up her chest.

"Those plans are up in the air for now." She patted her stomach. "It may take me a bit longer to finish the degree."

Guilt jabbed him. Here he was, trying to get her to do what he wanted to make life easier for him, without giving any thought to how this affected her plans. Was he that selfish? "Is there anything I can do?"

"Not unless you want to carry this baby for a while." She raised her eyebrows at him.

"Would that I could." His gaze went to her stomach. "But if you were upstairs, I could feed you, help you study."

She shook her head. "And don't you think having us living right upstairs would cramp your style? It might be hard to explain to your dates."

"There won't be any dates. I already told you there hasn't been anyone since…well, there hasn't been anyone else." He hated admitting his self-imposed drought, but maybe the reassurance would help change her mind. *That's mighty big of you, McBride. When did you get to be such an—*

"But that doesn't mean there won't be. You're not planning on being celibate the rest of your life, are you?" She raised her eyebrows at him.

Hell no. Huh, might be best to keep that to himself for now. He had better survival instincts than to continue any talk about sex, even if that's what he'd been hoping for when he'd spotted her on his front steps.

And how had this conversation deteriorated into a discussion of his sex life? Ellie had an uncanny ability to know what he was thinking and…yeah, best not dwell on that. She might be ignoring their chemistry, but it still sparked, at least for him. Although this might not be the best time to point that out. "How about we just get through telling the necessary people our news for now?"

"Sounds like a plan. I drank the rest of your milk."

"Oh-*kaay*…" The abrupt change of topic was enough to give him whiplash, but he'd take it. "We can go to the corner store and get more."

Her face brightened. "How far is it? This looks like a nice neighborhood to take a walk."

She wanted to take a walk? Hey, it was better than sitting here, *not* talking about sex. "Speaking of walking, where's your car? I didn't notice it out front."

Her gaze bounced away. "That's because it's not exactly out front."

"Oh? There are usually spots this time of the day. For instance, there was the one I took." He knew where this was going and he was going to enjoy taking it there. Teasing Ellie and watching her eyes spark always made him want to lean over and—huh, maybe this wasn't such a good idea.

"Well…there was only one and I thought… I thought—"

"Are you telling me you can't parallel park?" He leaned closer.

She scooted off the couch and went toward the bay windows. "Hey, it's not my fault. It's genetics. I'm missing the parallel parking gene."

"Genetics?" He stood and followed, as if tethered by invisible rope. "So does that mean this deficiency can be passed on? Isn't that something you should have warned me about?"

"Sorry?" She sucked on her bottom lip.

"Eh." He bit the inside of his cheek, trapping a smile. "Too late now. C'mon. Let's go to the corner store for milk." He puffed out his chest. "And while we're at it, I'll pull your car closer if you want, since I'm in possession of this awesome gene."

"Oh, brother." She rolled her eyes. "This corner store wouldn't by any chance have sandwiches or a deli?"

Was she serious? "You're hungry?"

"Starved."

"But I thought…" Liam tried to remember what Meg had been like when she was pregnant with Fiona and James, but his sister had hidden it or he'd been too blind to notice. Yeah, he was good at ignoring the obvious. Like with his ma. "If you say you're hungry, then I'll feed you."

She shook her head. "Yeah, not with what you've got on hand. I checked."

"You rummaged through my cupboards?" Was she really that hungry?

She scrunched up her nose. "Yes, Mother Hubbard, and I hate to break it to you, but they're pretty bare."

Who cared about what his kitchen cabinets did or did not contain when that pert, freckled nose was begging to be kissed?

"McBride?"

"Huh?" He shook his head, trying to get back on topic. He blamed his self-imposed eight-week period of celibacy for his lack of concentration.

She pointed to her mouth. "Food?"

It was his turn to wrinkle his nose. "You're serious about wanting to eat?"

"Oh, you mean because of the…in the bathroom?" She tilted her head toward the hallway and pulled a face.

He needed to proceed with caution if he wanted to avoid an argument or, worse, hurting her feelings. "You snapped at me for even suggesting coffee."

She fiddled with the neck of her sweater. "Yeah, about that… I lied. Sorry. The smell turns my stomach. I haven't been able to drink it or smell it for the past few weeks."

He glanced at the mug he'd set on the floor next to his recliner. "Do you want me to get rid of mine?"

Her eyes widened. "You mean you'd do that for me?"

"Of course." The coffee was probably cold by now, anyway. No great loss. He could make another cup when they got back from the store.

"That's so sweet," she gushed. "I can't tell you how much that would mean…you giving up coffee for the next seven months."

Wait…what? He opened his mouth but was incapable of forming words.

She patted his chest and hooted with laughter. "Sucker."

Yeah, he'd walked right into that one, but Ellie's laugh was worth it. Ellie made a lot of things worth it. He couldn't imagine going through this with anyone but her.

Chapter Nine

Ellie pondered the situation as they made their way to the corner store. His offer to be present when she broke the news to her parents had surprised and pleased her, and yet at the same time disappointed her. Had she expected more or were her hormones messing with her? Regardless, she had to admit she yearned for an admission that he'd missed her as much as she had him and that he regretted the no-strings-attached part of their arrangement. She needed to remember her vow to stay rooted in reality. *Learn to want what you have, not wish for what you don't.* Even if he'd proposed marriage, she wouldn't have accepted. She didn't want to end up like her mother with a kitchen table that had a lazy Susan but no one to use it. No shared meals or lively conversations. Now, her parents sat in front of the TV so they didn't have to talk and slept in separate bedrooms. They were like ghosts rattling around in the same house. Things hadn't been like that before her diagnosis and Ellie carried the burden of guilt. If she hadn't gotten cancer, would her mom and dad still be that loving, demonstrative couple she remembered from her pre-cancer days? The thought of doing something like that to her own child chilled her.

Instead of dwelling on a past she couldn't change, she pushed aside depressing thoughts to admire the differences and similarities in the homes lining the narrow street. Front porches and columns were common, although some had ornate railings and trim while many of the homeowners had boxed in the rococo trim using vinyl siding. She glanced back at Liam's and admired how his had only original details…except one. "How come yours is the only one with an external fire escape?"

"I'm the only fireman on the block."

Before she could comment, an elderly woman wearing a burgundy sweatshirt that said World's Greatest Grandma came toward them, dragging a fully loaded fold-up shopping cart.

Liam approached the woman. "Good morning, Mrs. Sullivan, looks like you could use some help getting that up your steps."

"Morning, Liam. I'm not the doddering old woman you seem to think, but since you're here…" She opened the gate on a chain-link fence surrounding a three-decker painted the same red and cream as Liam's.

"It's not your age but your beauty that attracts me, Mrs. Sullivan." He took the shopping cart from her.

"Oh, you are so full of it today, Liam McBride." She

leaned around him and smiled at Ellie. "Is that because you have this lovely young lady with you?"

"You wound me, Mrs. Sullivan, I assure you I'm totally sincere." He picked up the cart and set it on the wooden porch of the home.

Ellie's stomach tingled at Liam's solicitous behavior toward the older woman. It confirmed what she'd always known about his character.

"Aren't you going to introduce me?" The older woman clucked her tongue.

"Of course. Ellie Harding, this is Mrs. Sullivan." He motioned between the women.

"Fiddle faddle, I told you to call me Barbara." The woman poked him. "A pleasure to meet you, Ellie."

Ellie shook hands with the woman. "Same here."

"I haven't seen you around here before," the older woman said.

Ellie smiled at Barbara Sullivan. "That's because I live in Vermont. Loon Lake."

"Ah, that explains why Liam was gone so much this summer." The woman grinned and poked him again. "And here you were, telling me you were helping your sister."

He raised his hands, palms out. "I was. I helped them add a new master suite and family room."

"Why didn't you say something about Ellie when I tried to set you up with my granddaughter Chloe?"

He wanted her to live upstairs so he could take care of her? Yeah, right. And how would Chloe feel about a third or fourth wheel? Or maybe he wasn't interested in this Chloe because of their summer fling. Realistic? Maybe not, but it helped her to keep smiling at Chloe's grandmother.

"Shame on you for not telling me you already had someone in Vermont," the woman continued.

"That's because I—"

"We're not—"

Mrs. Sullivan looked from one to the other. "Uh-huh. Usually I see him and he's running or jogging or some such thing to keep fit for the ladies. You're not running today, Liam? But I guess if you've already been caught…"

"I'm not running because—" His brow knit and he hooked his thumb in Ellie's direction. "She's crap at keeping up."

"Apparently I'm crap at parallel parking, too," Ellie muttered. She didn't want to think about Liam and other women. And she certainly didn't want someone insinuating that she'd "caught" Liam as if she'd deliberately set a trap by getting pregnant.

"Don't worry about it, dear. I've lived on this street for fifty years and never learned to parallel park." Barbara Sullivan winked at Ellie.

"You don't own a car," Liam pointed out.

The woman shot him an affronted look. "What's that got to do with it?"

Liam heaved an exaggerated sigh. "Apparently nothing. Do you need help getting your shopping inside?"

"No, but thank you. Now you and your Ellie enjoy your walk." The older woman made a shooing motion.

"She seems nice," Ellie said as Liam shut the gate with a clang of metal.

Liam nodded. "Mmm, she is…for the most part."

"Sorry if she assumed that we were…well, that we were together." Good grief, why was she apologizing? This baby wasn't an immaculate conception—even if that's what she'd love to be able tell her dad. Not to mention all the elderly ladies at the church next time she volunteered at the weekly luncheon. *Oh, grow up, those women were all young once.* "But then, we're going to have a baby so I guess you can't get more together than that."

He frowned. "Are you saying—"

"I'm not saying anything. Like I said—huh, well, I guess I am saying *something*." *Damn hormones.* "But I'm not pressing you for anything."

"For God's sake, Ellie, I'll do my share."

The rational part of her brain, when it still worked, knew that expecting him to move would be as crazy as him expecting her to move. Offering her a place to live might solve the problem of distance for him, but being on the periphery of Liam's life was not what she wanted. She wanted to *be* Liam's life. She wanted what Meg and Riley, or Mary and Brody, had. Yeah, that right there was the problem. "That might be difficult since you'll be here and I'll be in Loon Lake."

"Careful." He placed a hand under her elbow and pointed to the uneven sidewalk.

"I'm pregnant, not blind." She cringed at her own waspish tone and blinked to hold back tears. Since when did she have the power to make people react or feel the way she wanted? If she had that power, she'd have put her parents' in-name-only marriage back together.

"But with my schedule, I can get ninety-six hours off, unless I take extra shifts. That's four days."

"I know how long ninety-six hours is." And she knew how long it took to drive from his place to hers. How involved could she honestly expect him to be? She might have regularly scheduled hours at her job but it wasn't as if she was always able to leave on time. Same for Liam if they got called out before quitting time; she knew he couldn't just leave.

He blew out his breath. "Are you trying to start a fight?"

"No." *Liar.* "Maybe."

He stopped, placed his hands on her shoulders and turned her to face him. His gaze scanned her face, his blue eyes full of concern. "What can I do to get your mind off fighting?"

An image popped into her head. Yeah, like she was going to suggest something like *that*. She chose option two. "You could try feeding me."

Was that disappointment on his face? Hmm, seems his mind had gone there, too. *Join the club.* But now was not a good time to muddle things with sex, her sensible half pointed out. But it could be so much fun, her daring half argued.

At the moment hunger was the deciding factor. Those cookies and milk she'd eaten while Liam was in the shower seemed like ages ago. "Is that pizza I smell?"

"There's a small place around the corner."

Her stomach growled. "Can we go there?"

"It's barely ten and that place is a grease pit." He frowned.

"And your point is?"

"Grease can't be good for…for—" his Adam's apple bobbed "—the baby."

"For your information, grease is a food group." Despite her insistence, a pizza didn't hold the same appeal as it had a few minutes ago. And yet a feeling of dissatisfaction made her persist. "Are you going to feed me or not?"

"Fine. We can go to there if you really want or we can go to the store and get milk, some stuff for sandwiches and maybe some fruit or salad."

She already regretted acting so disagreeable. Why did being with Liam again make her feel so contrary? She was blaming her body's reaction to his touch. "Fruit and salad? Who are you and what have you done with the Liam I know?"

"Smart aleck." He dropped his hands, but not before giving her shoulders a gentle squeeze and dropping a kiss on the end of her nose.

She fell into step beside him. "Actually, sandwiches sound better than pizza."

He draped an arm around her shoulders. "If you insist on empty calories after sandwiches, I have some snickerdoodles from Meg and—"

"Had," she interrupted.

"Huh?"

"Had, as in past tense. I…uh, found them while I was tidying up. Why do you think I drank the rest of your milk?"

"Huh." He rubbed his chin. "I guess my cupboards weren't as bare as you claimed."

"Don't push it, McBride."

"I wouldn't dream of it, Harding."

A bell dinged and a cashier greeted them when they entered the neighborhood store, reminding Ellie of the Whatleys' Loon Lake General Store; Liam's offer of an apartment in his building flashed through her mind, but she just as quickly discarded it. They'd muddle through somehow, especially since their work schedules gave them both stretches with days off.

The cashier who'd greeted Liam by name as they entered immediately engaged him in a discussion of the baseball playoffs. Listening to the two debate a controversial ruling at second base, Ellie wandered to the rear of the store and a well-stocked deli.

"Morning." A woman with short dark hair and a Red Sox baseball cap stood behind the deli counter. She hitched her chin toward the front of the store. "You a friend of Liam's?"

"Something like that." *Friends who just happen to be having a baby.* Being friends with Liam was easy; resisting his crooked smile and quick wit was a different matter. Sleeping with him again would only complicate things. *But it sure would be fun.*

"What can I get you?" the clerk prompted, tightening the ties on her bibbed apron.

"Hmm…" Ellie's gaze traveled up and down the display case. She never knew what her stomach was going to accept. One minute she craved something, the next it made her gag. Her appetite was as mercurial as her moods.

"Liam's partial to the honey ham," the clerk suggested.

"Okay, that sounds good." At least he could eat it if her stomach revolted. "And some provolone."

Liam approached carrying a loaf of white bread and Ellie shook her head. "I'm not eating that."

He held the package up and eyed it. "What? You don't like bread now?"

She liked bread but was trying to eat healthy, or at least healthier. She was going to be someone's mom and needed to set a good example. "Don't they have whole wheat or twelve grain? Did you learn nothing from me this summer?"

"Yeah, I learned to hide my junk food," he said, and rolled his eyes.

A suspicious snickering sound came from the other side of the counter and Ellie glanced over. The woman's back was to them but her shoulders were shaking.

"Glad you find my being forced to eat healthier funny, Mrs. O'Brien," Liam said in a dry tone.

The woman turned around. "It's about time you settled down with a woman who is interested in taking good care of you, Liam."

"We're not—"

"Oh, we're just—"

The woman winked as she handed over two packages wrapped in white butcher paper. "I sliced it the way you like."

Liam was still stuffing his wallet into his back pocket after paying when Ellie poked into the bag and pulled out a package of chocolate-covered graham crackers. What the hell? He shook his head. She'd given him grief over some stupid bread and she was chowing down on more cookies. He made a mental note to ask Riley if pregnancy made women unreasonable.

Ellie stuck the package of cookies under her arm and held out her hands. "I can carry some of that."

He lifted the bags out of reach as they exited the store. "I got it."

She glanced back as they turned the corner onto his street. "See? That's why I could never move in upstairs."

He turned his head. What was she seeing that he wasn't? The street looked the same as it had when they'd arrived. "I don't follow what you're getting at."

"They assumed we were together."

"Umm…we were."

She shook her head vigorously. "I mean *together* together."

Maybe he was the one losing his mind. He chose silence.

"Once my pregnancy starts showing, people would be asking all sorts of questions and making assumptions."

"Assumptions? Like that we'd had sex?" Damn his big mouth. "C'mon, they'll do all that in Loon Lake."

"Yes, but, judgment or not, they'll also be there for me if I ever need help." Her lower lip came out in a pout.

Ooh, what he wanted to do with that sexy lower lip. Even in a pout, that mouth called to him. "This is Dorchester today, not in the 1950s. No one is going to judge you."

"That's what you think. How come you never went out with Mrs. Sullivan's granddaughter?" she asked as they passed Barbara Sullivan's three-decker.

"Because I have to live on this street." Evidently they were done talking about moving. He'd bide his time, but he wasn't giving up. Huh…he should be relieved she wasn't demanding all sorts of concessions from him, but the idea of her being so far away from him, in Vermont, annoyed him.

"But you said you always part on friendly terms with women you date. No harm, no foul," Ellie said.

"You wanna try explaining that to Grandmother Sullivan?"

She nodded. "Good point."

"And for your information, I'm not some sort of serial dater." However, he'd had enough relationships to understand the signals leading to the point where women began uttering accusations like "emotionally unavailable" and ended things before that happened. He liked to end on good terms. If the relationship progressed to the point of using those phrases, the inevitable parting could become acrimonious. He never wanted anything like that for himself and Ellie. Is that why he'd hesitated getting involved with her in the past? Of course the no-strings-attached thing hadn't exactly worked in his favor. He glanced at Ellie. Or had it? Could a child keep them together?

"You have to admit, you've dated a lot of women," she was saying.

"True, but they've been spread out over sixteen years. Never two at once and I never poached." Why did he feel the need to defend his dating history? He never had in the past.

They were back at his house and he shifted the bags so he could reach his keys.

Ellie reached over and grabbed a bag. "Here, let me take one of those."

Their fingers brushed and there was that spark he'd remembered but had tried to deny for the past two months. He needed to ignore it if he was going to put Ellie back into the friend zone. That was where she needed to be if they were going to work on a partnership for the sake of their child.

After lunch in the living room, Ellie brought her empty plate into the kitchen and paused in the doorway. Liam's hair had flopped over his forehead as he bent over to load the dishwasher and her fingers twitched with the need to brush it back. Their summer fling was over, and pregnant or not, she didn't have the right to touch him with such tenderness, as much as she ached to do so.

"I should leave soon to beat the traffic." She handed him her plate and grabbed another chocolate-covered graham cracker from the bag on the counter.

"Leave? Already?" He glanced up and frowned. "Why don't you stay tonight? You look beat."

"I'll be fine. I didn't plan to stay, so I didn't bring anything with me." She contemplated her cookie before taking a bite. The thought of packing an overnight bag had occurred to her, but she didn't like the message that would send. Whether to Liam or to herself, she wasn't sure. Maybe both.

"We can go and get you whatever you need. Boston happens to be a very cosmopolitan city. Stores, restaurants, hospitals—"

"Don't start with me." While she believed in coparenting, living in such proximity to him without sharing his life would be impossible. She wanted it all. She was sick of being in the friend zone with guys. Was it too much to want one who saw her as a friend and a lover, a life partner, a guy whose heart sped up at the sight of her? Someone who was interested in something other than her bowling score or batting average? One who wouldn't bury himself in work when life got tough?

Her father used work to bury his emotions brought on by the uncertainty of her cancer. But blocking out his emotions meant he couldn't deal with his wife's, either. Ellie couldn't blame it all on her dad. She understood not everyone could handle all those emotions surrounding such a diagnosis. Of course, she also understood her mother feeling abandoned by the man who was supposed to be there for her in sickness as well as health. Trying not to take sides meant her own relationship with her parents was strained and not as close as it had once been.

He slammed the dishwasher door shut. "If you insist on going back this afternoon, I'm driving. I don't want you falling asleep at the wheel."

"Hello? I'm an ER nurse. I know better than that." If a brisk walk around the block didn't work, she would think of something that made her spitting mad. Angry people tended to be more alert. If that failed, she'd pull into the first rest area.

He leaned against the counter, his arms folded over his chest, his feet crossed at the ankles. "Either stay here with me tonight or I drive you back to Vermont. That's the deal."

She grabbed another cookie. She could argue with him, but what would that accomplish? And she really was dead on her feet and not looking forward to the drive to Loon Lake. Now that she'd delivered her news the nervous energy was gone, replaced with the usual afternoon fatigue. "But how will you get back?"

"One of the guys can drive my truck to pick me up."

"Were you able to get enough sleep on your shift?"

He nodded. "Yeah, a couple callouts but not bad."

"Okay, you can drive me back." Spending more time together was important if they were going to co-parent.

His head jerked back as he studied her. That devilishly sexy grin appeared, the one that deepened the grooves bracketing his mouth. The one that threatened her resolve to not throw herself at him. The one she was powerless to resist.

When he opened his mouth, she pointed her cookie at him. "Don't crow. It's not attractive."

"Says you." He straightened up and pulled away from the counter, his light blue eyes gleaming with mischief. "Let me get some things so *I* won't get caught short spending the night."

"Fine, but if you stay at my place, you'll be sleeping on the couch," she called to his retreating back.

He turned and began walking backward. His low chuckle said he was remembering the things they'd done on her couch. Damn. Now she had all those images in her head.

Those pesky snippets were still playing like movie trailers in her head as they drove through the narrow, winding streets of Boston.

"What can I say to convince you to move here?" he asked.

Tell me you love me and can't live without me. Tell me I'm the most important person in your life. Tell me you're in this for the good times and *the tough ones.* "Nothing. It ain't gonna happen."

He glanced over at her as he took the on-ramp to the interstate and sped up to blend into traffic. "The upstairs apartments are just as nice as mine. You said you liked it and you could decorate any way you wanted."

"I'm sure it's very nice, but I want to stay in Loon Lake." There, she wouldn't have to watch Liam living his life with her on the periphery. In Boston, she'd be cut off from friends. If she were truly already a part of Liam's life, giving up Loon Lake wouldn't be that hard. But she wasn't and it mattered. "You said Meg picked Loon Lake to live in to raise Fiona. I want the same things for my child. I have nothing against where you live. Your street is very nice and if Mrs. Sullivan is anything to go by, the people are nice, too. But I enjoy small-town living for all its inherent problems."

"Okay, I won't press."

"Thanks," she said, but she had a feeling the subject wasn't dead, just dormant. But she'd enjoy the respite. "I love the idea of our child growing up close to Meg's kids."

He nodded and sighed. "There is that."

"Just think, another seven or eight years and Fiona will be able to babysit." Family ties were another reason to stay in Loon Lake. Her child would have ties to the town and its people the same way she did.

"Fiona babysitting. Lord help us all." He chuckled.

Ellie laughed and yawned. She settled back against the seat. It seemed like she ran out of steam every afternoon, no matter how much sleep she'd gotten the night before. And due to her pending trip, she hadn't gotten a whole lot last night.

Despite her pregnancy fatigue, her mind wouldn't turn off. Yes, she wanted to do what was best for her child and she was convinced Liam would be a wonderful father. Not to mention, the rest of the McBrides would surround her child with family and love.

Was it selfish to want some of that for herself, too?

Chapter Ten

Liam had meant what he said. He wouldn't keep pressing her about moving, but he hated having two hundred miles between them. What was he supposed to do in an emergency? What if Ellie or his child needed him? He didn't want to be so far away from either of them.

He spared a quick glance over at his sleeping passenger and grinned. As much as he enjoyed Ellie's company, he was glad she was getting the rest she so obviously needed, judging by the circles under her eyes.

Yep, not letting her drive was the right decision. She'd make a great mother, and surely Ellie could undo anything he might inadvertently screw up. The enormity of the situation was sinking in and he must be getting used to the idea of being a father because he didn't panic each time the thought ran through his head. Well, that whole not-panicking thing was relative.

Before they'd left, he'd decided telling his sister right away made sense and Ellie had agreed. He'd hate for Meg to hear the news from someone else. Slowing Ellie's car, he turned onto the driveway to his sister's house.

The driveway leading to Meg and Riley's began as a shared driveway, then it forked off into two. Her home was set back about one hundred yards from the main road. The house was surrounded by towering trees on three sides, and if not for the other home across the front yard from theirs, Meg and Riley would be all alone in the woods. On the other side of the trees, the lake was visible only during winter.

A swing set, sandbox and bicycle leaning against the open porch announced this was a family home. At one time, Liam had urged Meg to go in with him to purchase the Boston three-decker, but she'd been adamant about wanting a real yard for Fiona and his wasn't much more than a postage stamp. He saw now that she'd made the right choice. Even before Riley returned to claim his small family, Meg had done the best thing for her and Fiona by moving here. Was that how Ellie felt?

He parked next to his sister's car and shut off the engine. Reaching over, he shook Ellie's shoulder. "Hey, sleepyhead, we're here."

Ellie blinked and sat up straight. She wiped a hand across her mouth and groaned. "Was I drooling?"

"Only the last hour or so." He took the key from the ignition.

"Why didn't you wake me?"

"Because then I couldn't razz you about drooling."

"Brat." She unbuckled her seat belt and scrambled out of the car. "Let's get this over with."

He got out and followed her onto the porch. Leaning down, he squeezed her hand and whispered, "Think of this as a practice run before we tell your parents."

Ellie had barely knocked when the front door was flung open and Meg, dressed in jeans and an oversize sweatshirt, greeted them.

"I thought I heard a car pull in." Meg gave Liam a questioning look as he hugged her and kissed her cheek. "This is a surprise."

"I hope we didn't come at a bad time," Ellie said. She was chewing her bottom lip.

"No, no. Come in." Meg waved them in and led them through the original cozy living room to the kitchen. "I hope you don't mind, but I have cookies in the oven and don't want them to burn."

Liam glanced around, surprised by the silence. With two kids and a dog, Meg and Riley's home was usually a lot more boisterous. "Where is everyone?"

"James is taking a nap and Riley had the day off, so he did the school run to get Fiona, and the dog jumped in the truck with him. He texted that they were going to stop at the lake to let Mangy and Fiona blow off some steam before coming home." Meg pulled out a cookie tin and set it on the table. "Sit."

Liam reached for the tin. "Snickerdoodles?"

"Manners much?" Meg swatted his arm. "Let Ellie have some first. These cookies are Riley and Fiona's favorites. They already gave me grief for taking half the batch to you last time I made them."

"I didn't forget, but *someone* got into my stash and ate the rest." He scowled at Ellie, doing his best to hide a grin.

Ellie glared back and pulled out a chair. "Hey, there weren't that many."

"Want some coffee to go with the cookies?" Meg asked, giving them quizzical looks.

"No," Liam practically shouted, remembering Ellie's aversion to the smell. Clearing his throat, he searched for a calmer tone. "No, thanks. Milk is fine."

Meg frowned but pulled a gallon of milk out of the refrigerator and reached into the cabinet for glasses.

Ellie sat down and grabbed a cookie while Liam poured milk for everyone.

Meg leaned toward Ellie. "I knew you were going to Boston, but you didn't tell me you were bringing trouble back with you."

Ellie broke a cookie in half and dipped it into her milk. "I didn't know he was coming. He insisted. You know how bossy he can get."

"You know I can hear you two," he grumbled before shoving a cookie in his mouth. Meg's body language told him she suspected something was up and they weren't going to be able to hold her off for much longer.

He swallowed his cookie and made eye contact with Ellie, checking to make sure she was ready. "We, uh, have something we need to tell you."

Meg did a fist pump. "What's up? I know how you clicked over the summer. You two getting married?"

Liam nearly choked on his milk. "No!"

"Ass." Meg punched his arm, sending milk sloshing over the top of his glass and onto his hand.

"Language?" Liam used a napkin to wipe off his hand and wet sleeve. He tried to act affronted but he regretted his knee-jerk answer. Looking at Ellie's face, he knew he shouldn't have said anything, even if that was his first reaction.

"You deserved it and the kids can't hear me." Meg turned to Ellie and shook her head. "I apologize for my—"

"It's okay," Ellie interrupted. "We don't have any plans like that."

Liam felt like the ass his sister had called him. Ellie was smiling, but her eyes were overly bright. Damn, he'd made her cry twice in one day. He reached across the table and touched Ellie's hand. "I didn't mean it the way it sounded."

"I know." Ellie cleared her throat. "I'm... That is, we're having a baby."

"A baby?" Meg's eyes grew wide. "Wow... Uh, I mean congratulations. That's...serious."

"Oh, we're not—"

"We aren't—"

"Uh, guys." Meg's gaze bounced from one to the other, shaking her head. "Having a baby together is pretty serious."

Seeing Ellie's flushed face, Liam sent his sister a nonverbal warning, hoping their sibling connection would say what he wasn't, even if he didn't know exactly what he was trying to say. "Yes, it's serious, but we're friends who will also happen to be parents together."

Meg nodded, but her expression screamed skepticism. "Does Dad know?"

Liam squeezed his eyes shut. "Not yet."

"At least you're in a better situation than I was when I had to confess," Meg said.

Liam groaned. "It's not like I can use my age as an excuse."

"He'll get over it. Doris has been a good influence on him and she'll be thrilled. She loves babies," Meg said, and turned her attention to Ellie. "I'm happy for both of you and excited to be an aunt. I never thought I'd have that honor. Riley's an only child and, well, Liam, he's—"

"Sitting right here, sister dear," he interrupted, raising his eyebrows.

Meg rolled her eyes. "I'm excited to be an aunt and for Fiona and James and this new baby to have a cousin."

Before Ellie could respond, Meg rushed on, "Too bad you won't be here in Loon Lake. We could be like pregnant sisters."

Ellie shook her head. "Oh, but I have no plans to move anywhere."

Liam ground his molars. Ellie's pregnancy wasn't planned but it was a reality and he didn't appreciate being shut out of major decisions, which might happen if Ellie stayed in Loon Lake. What other explanation was there for his caveman behavior around her?

Meg glanced at him with a *help me out here* look. He responded with a quick shake of his head.

"That's even better," Meg said. "We can be pregnant together. I think Mary and Brody are starting to think about giving Elliott a brother or sister. Wouldn't that be fun? Our kids could form their own play group."

Ellie pulled her hand free of Liam's. She leaned over and gave Meg a hug. "I'd love that. Our kids are going to be family and I want them to be close."

"Yeah, you're getting to be an old pro at this, sis," Liam said.

"Liam!" Ellie poked him with her elbow.

Meg laughed. "What can I say? Riley and I—"

"Riley and I what?" another voice came from the doorway to the kitchen.

Riley greeted Liam and Ellie as he walked over to Meg and leaned down to give her a kiss.

Meg put her arm around her husband's waist. "Where's Fiona?"

"Dang, I knew I forgot something." He leaned in for another kiss. When he finally pulled away, he said, "She's outside with the dog. Mangy's paws got all dirty and I didn't think you'd want muddy prints all over your floors."

"Mmm. Good call." Meg gave him a dreamy look.

Liam brought his hand up and covered his eyes. "Guys, company here."

Despite his joking complaints, something sharp poked him when he saw how happy his little sister was in her marriage. He was glad, he truly was, but seeing it made him realize what he was lacking. Could he and Ellie build that sort of life together? Whenever he imagined his future, Ellie was front and center.

"Oh, yes." Meg patted Riley's chest. "Wait until you hear Liam and Ellie's news. They're having a baby."

"Really? Congratulations." Riley clapped Liam on the back. "When's the big day?"

"Uh, we don't know yet… Ellie hasn't gone to the doctor." Liam looked to Ellie.

Riley shook his head. "I didn't mean the baby due date, I meant— Oomph."

Meg's jab to the ribs effectively silenced Riley, and she turned to explain. "Ellie and my brother are going to be…" She glanced at Liam but didn't wait for confirmation before saying, "They're going to be friends who have a baby together."

Before anyone could say anything else, Fiona burst into the kitchen. "Mommy, I taught Mangy to catch the Frisbee. 'Cept he won't bring it back to me."

"That can be lesson two," Meg said. "Did you tie him to the outdoor run before coming in?"

"Uh-huh, I tied him so he can't run away or run into the woods and get lost. Uncle Liam, I didn't know you were here. Where's your truck?" The redheaded dynamo, a mini Meg, barreled over to Liam and hugged him.

"I came with Nurse Ellie." He gave his niece a bear hug.

"Are you sick?" She tilted her head back and looked up at him.

He chucked her under her chin. "No, Ellie and I are friends, just like she and your mom are friends. We came in her car to visit you."

"How come you came to visit me?" she asked.

Liam laughed. "I meant—"

A baby's cry came from somewhere in the house.

"I'll go get him," Riley said.

"Thanks." Meg pulled him back with a hand on his shirt and gave him another kiss.

Fiona pointed at her parents. "Uh-oh, Mommy, you better be careful. Uncle Liam said all that kissing stuff is what leads to all our babies."

Liam groaned and rolled his eyes. The little blabbermouth. He just couldn't catch a break today.

"Oh, he did, did he?" Meg gave him a stern look. "Fiona, why don't you take Ellie outside and show her how you taught Mangy to catch the Frisbee. Maybe Auntie Ellie knows how to make Mangy bring the Frisbee back."

Fiona scrunched up her face. "Aren't you and Uncle Liam coming?"

"Yes, we'll be out in just a minute."

Riley chuckled and clapped Liam on the shoulder before leaving the kitchen. "Good luck."

Liam watched Fiona take Ellie's hand as they went outside and wished like heck he was going with them.

Once the door shut behind them, he turned to his sister. "You gonna rip me a new one now?"

"Nope." Meg shook her head. "But I will say that how many kids Riley and I have is none of your business, just like whether or not you marry Ellie for the sake of *your* child is none of mine."

"Maybe we shouldn't have stayed for supper with my parents," Ellie said when Liam yawned as they drove to her apartment later that evening. He hadn't had the benefit of a nap as she had and he'd spent the better part of the afternoon chasing the dog to retrieve the Frisbee for Fiona to throw again. "I forgot you just came off a shift this morning."

After leaving Riley and Meg's, they'd stopped at her parents' home to break the news. Liam had suggested it, likening it to ripping off a bandage. Faster was better, he'd suggested. She would have preferred maybe another day to gather her courage but didn't want to take a chance they'd hear it from someone else.

But if she were honest, having to tell her parents she was pregnant hadn't been what bothered her the most about going to her childhood home. When they'd arrived, her father had been in his basement workshop, where he spent most of his time. As if he wasn't a part of what went on above those stairs. Her mom was in the stark white living room, where footprints didn't mar the carpet. Ellie could remember when the house was full of noise and clutter. No, it was the memories being dredged up. She could remember the laughter, the loving glances and tender touches between her parents before she'd gotten sick. She'd taken all of that for granted when she'd had it, thinking it would last forever. Now they were more like polite strangers. They'd remained married because her mother believed that's what you did. The marriage was in place but their relationship had withered and died.

"It's okay. Your mom's a good cook and I slept some last night. Plus, I have time to sleep before the extra shift I mentioned at supper." He glanced over at her and grinned. "Besides, I wasn't about to argue with your dad when he extended the invitation."

She picked at a hangnail. Despite her mom's initial concern over the fact that they had no marriage plans, she was looking forward to being a grandmother. Her dad had started to say something about the risk to her health but her mother shut him up with a stern look and a muttered "It's not our decision." When her dad had suggested Liam join him in the den while she helped her mom load the dishwasher she'd wanted to throw herself into the doorway to block their exit. And her objection wasn't solely because of her dad's sexist attitude toward chores. If she wanted to know something, she needed to ask. "What did my father say to you when you two went into the den?"

"Oh, you know..." He shrugged. "The usual guy talk."

She rubbed her chest. Had he already put her back into the *one of the guys* category? "You forget, I'm a woman." She managed a small laugh. "What's the usual guy talk?"

He took his eyes off the road to give her an assessing glance. "Whether or not the Patriots can go all the way again this year. You okay?"

"Fine." She glanced at the passing scenery as they drove across town. They might not be in any sort of committed relationship, but having a baby together was pretty important. Important enough to share things. "So you're going to tell me that you and my dad went into the den to talk about football?"

He blew out his breath. "It's all in the subtext."

Okay, so maybe they did talk sports. "So my dad didn't come right out and threaten your manhood?"

"Don't go there. Please." Liam winced and glanced down at his lap.

"Sorry," she said, and bit the inside of her cheek to keep from laughing.

"No, you're not." He huffed out his breath. "Your dad was subtle. He didn't drag out a shotgun to polish or anything like that. He did, however, stress that it was important for me to be an involved father and that included financial support. I assured him I'd do my share."

"My mother said maybe we should have started out a little slower, like maybe getting a dog first...see how that worked out." Her mother had been torn between rejoicing at having a grandchild and being concerned over her still-single status.

Liam chuckled. "There's still time...to get a dog, that is. I could check with Riley. I know he researched the one he got for Fiona so it wouldn't aggravate Meg's asthma."

"Yeah, Meg said he was careful before getting it."

"And then he went and spoiled it by letting Fiona name it Mangy."

She choked out a sob of half laughter. "How would we take care of it? With both our jobs, we—" She shifted in her seat. "Oh, God, Liam, how can we be parents if we can't even take care of a dog?"

He pulled into the driveway that led to her rental apartment, but didn't go all the way up to the place. Putting the car into Park, he grabbed her hand and gave it a supportive squeeze. "First of all, we don't have a dog, so quit worrying about a hypothetical situation. You're going to be a great mom. And we have plenty of time to work out the logistics."

"I'm going to be a single mother. Who knows if I'm going to be able to finish everything for my NP certification? That means I can't give up my current job." She hated that she sounded as if she were whining. Her job, while sometimes stressful, was something she enjoyed and it paid enough to support her and a baby; she had it a lot better than most. Plus Liam said he would be stepping up and she knew he was a man of his word. Poor Meg had had to do the single-mother thing for years before Riley came back into her life. Ellie knew Liam had done what he could to help Meg, but she'd still been alone at the end of the day.

"No one is asking you to give up your career goals. We'll work out our schedules."

She opened her mouth to ask how he could be so cavalier, but shut it without saying anything. He was being supportive and didn't need her finding fault. "You're right."

"What did you say?"

She huffed out a sigh. "I said you're right."

"Can I get that in writing?"

"Don't push it."

He laughed and squeezed her hand once more before letting go and driving the rest of the way to her place.

The motion-sensitive lights came on as they approached the three-car garage.

"Do you park in the garage?" Liam asked.

"I haven't been, because there's no inside access to the apartment. Of course, I may rethink that in the middle of winter if the owner of the main house still hasn't moved in."

Liam parked her Subaru and she led the way up the exterior stairs located on one side of the garage and unlocked the door. Her place was perfect for a single woman. But where would she put all the paraphernalia needed for a baby? Even a high chair would be a tight fit for the kitchen.

The *thump* of a duffel bag hitting the floor interrupted her thoughts, and hands came to rest on her shoulders as if he'd been able to follow her silent thoughts. She leaned back into Liam's warmth and strength.

"It's going to be okay," he said as his fingers massaged the kinks caused by the day's tension.

She tilted her head back and stared up at him. He had the beginnings of a five o'clock shadow. He'd let his facial hair grow out a bit on his four-day rotation, but he would have to be clean-shaven when he went back on duty to allow the secure suction his respirator needed. She knew so many things about him and yet they now felt like mere details. "How come I'm the one freaking out and you're the voice of reason?"

His arms went around her and he leaned down and kissed the tip of her nose. "Just abiding by the rules."

"Rules?" She turned in the shelter of his arms. It felt so good to be there, to lean her head against his chest and listen to his steady heartbeat.

"I've decided only one of us is allowed to freak out at a time. I'm counting on you to be the voice of reason when I panic." He gave her a quick squeeze. "Whaddaya say? Deal?"

She hugged him but quickly stepped back, making sure the contact didn't last too long. Like ripping off a bandage. She didn't want him to think she was throwing herself at him—even if that was what she wanted to do. "Deal."

Chapter Eleven

Liam stooped to pick up his duffel from the kitchen floor. Ellie's message was clear that she'd put him back in the no-sex friend zone. But that was good...wasn't it? Friendship was what he'd been telling himself he wanted. Anything more than that meant opening up, making himself vulnerable, which he was pretty sure Ellie would demand, and he was just as sure he would refuse. How could he tell her his concerns about the threat of being left a single parent if the cancer returned? He'd look like a selfish chump saying something like that. Shaking his head at the thoughts dancing around in his head, he followed her into her living area.

Her apartment, around six hundred square feet, was half the size of his place. He remembered all the stuff his sister had needed for Fiona; there'd been baby gear everywhere in the traditional Cape Cod–style house he'd been sharing with his dad and sister. After his ma had been diagnosed, he'd moved back to his childhood home, ostensibly to help, but frankly he'd welcomed being closer to his family during that time. He'd bought his three-decker after his mother's death, hoping Meg would join him, but she'd insisted on moving to the family's vacation home in Loon Lake.

He glanced around. Where would Ellie put all the baby stuff? Ellie was compulsively neat and organized, even keeping her possessions to a minimum in the apartment to avoid clutter.

"Are you going to have enough room here?" If she intended to move, he and Riley could help, maybe even scrounge up a few other guys. She didn't need to be lifting things in her condition.

"You've stayed over before. It was never a—"

"No, I meant after the…" He swallowed. "After the baby comes."

"I told you already, I'm not moving into your upstairs apartment." She opened the linen closet next to the bathroom in the short hall leading to the bedroom.

"That's not why I said it." That was still his idea of the best scenario but he wasn't going to argue with her tonight. She looked tired and his conscience pricked him. Rest was what she needed. "If you decide to move to somewhere else in Loon Lake, Riley and I can help. I'm sure we can find plenty of people willing to do the heavy lifting for you."

She stepped back from the open closet, a stack of sheets and a blanket in her arms. "Right now, I'm not sure I have the energy to pack and move."

He lifted the bedding from her arms. Would the fact that she'd had cancer make a difference to the pregnancy? Could all that she'd gone through have an impact on her ability carry the baby safely to term? "Is that normal? Should we go to the doctor to be sure?"

"Fatigue is perfectly normal in the beginning."

"Like the throwing up?" He crushed the sheets in his grip.

"Yeah, I'm afraid that is, too." She frowned and snatched one of the sheets from his grasp. "Hopefully, both will improve in about a month. I understand the second trimester is actually rather pleasant. Don't you remember any of this from your sister?"

"Like I said, she was good at hiding it the first time and I didn't live with her the second time around." Or he was just that good at ignoring the obvious.

"Given the circumstances for her first pregnancy, I guess that makes sense." She reached for the sheet in his arms and began to put it on the couch. He set the rest of the bedding on the coffee table and began to help her.

"So you were serious when you said I had to sleep on the couch." He raised his eyebrows as he tucked the sheet between the cushions and the back of the couch.

"You can always sleep at your sister's, if she'll have you." Ellie slipped a pillowcase over the pillow.

Okay, she put him in his place. But hey, a guy could try. "I think it would get a little crowded."

"Crowded? I thought that's what the new addition was for." She punched the pillow.

He winced as he watched her treatment of his pillow. "I was thinking crowded more in terms of people and dog, rather than space."

Sighing, she fluffed the pillow out. "What do you think this place is gonna be like once we have a baby?"

"Why do you think I suggested moving into my upstairs apartment?" He regretted the words as soon as they found air. Pressing his point right now was counterproductive.

"Give it a rest, Liam." Ellie smoothed out a blanket over the sheet and arranged the pillow at one end of the sofa. "Well, good night. I hope you get a good night's sleep."

"So you're not going to take pity on me?" he called to her retreating back.

"That puppy-dog face of yours won't get you anywhere, McBride."

"Hey, you weren't even looking."

After she had shut the bedroom door, Liam stripped down to his boxer briefs and got between the covers on the sofa.

A short time later, he jackknifed into a sitting position and glanced around. He sat and listened to see what had awakened him up from a sound sleep. He was accustomed to sleeping around a dozen other guys during shifts at the fire station, so noises in the night didn't usually bother him.

"Are you okay?" he asked Ellie as she came down the short hall from her bedroom.

She nodded. "I got up to use the bathroom and decided to get a drink of water. I'm sorry if I woke you, but I'm not used to having someone here with me."

"It's okay. I just wanted to be sure you weren't sick again." And he wanted to say stuff, but he wasn't even sure what it was he wanted to say, let alone how to say it. And, man, wasn't that messed up?

She shook her head. "No. That's mostly in the mornings but that's not hard and fast."

He nodded. "That's good."

"Glad you think so." Her tone was dry.

Aw, man, could he not catch a break? "I didn't mean… I only meant—"

"You're making this way too easy." She thumped him on the shoulder and grinned.

"And yet you keep doing it," he grumbled, and rubbed his shoulder, but his actions were for effect. She wasn't angry and he was grateful. He certainly hadn't meant to piss her off. "I'm trying to be supportive."

"And I appreciate it, but you don't need to hover."

"I don't hover." And even if he did, who could blame him? Ellie was pregnant with his child. He was doing his best to hold it all together and not let his panic show.

"Well…good night. And sorry for waking you."

"Don't worry about it."

She went back into the bedroom and he sank down on the couch and punched the pillow. He had just stretched out when a noise had him opening his eyes. Ellie was standing next to the couch.

He sat up. "What's the matter?"

She chewed on her bottom lip. "Umm…that couch isn't very comfortable."

"I've had worse."

She reached out her hand toward him and he grabbed it. Still unsure of what was happening, he frowned. "Ellie?"

"I don't want to send the wrong signal but…" She tugged on his hand. She waved her free hand toward the bedroom. "We can share, right? I'm talking platonic."

Relief swept through him as he grabbed his pillow with his free hand and let her lead him to the bedroom. Spending the night in the same bed with Ellie, even in a platonic sense, was important. He couldn't pinpoint why. Too much had happened today to make sense of the jumble of emotions. He just knew he wanted to be as close as possible to her.

Ellie's first thought upon awakening was Liam. She lay in his arms and it wasn't a dream. Oh, yeah, she'd invited him to sleep in the bed. At the time she'd fallen asleep he'd been way over on his side of the bed and she on hers. Now they were huddled together in the middle as if their bodies had taken over while they slept.

Sighing, she burrowed closer, intent on enjoying the moment. This time of year, the mornings could be cool, so waking to warmth was unusual.

"Ellie?" he murmured near her ear.

"Mmm?" She huddled closer.

He cleared his throat. "Could you not do that?"

She moved again, shimmying closer, then scolding herself. What was she doing? She shouldn't tease unless she intended to follow through. Maybe sex wouldn't be a total disaster. After all, she couldn't get pregnant again. She shifted.

"Yeah, that," he groaned, his voice tight.

"Sorry." She scooted away and turned to face him. Did she want to do this? "Truly, I am sorry. That wasn't nice."

"Not unless you plan to—" His cell phone rang before he could finish. He heaved an exasperated sigh. "That's my dad's ringtone."

Ellie was already scooting to the other side of the bed. Interrupted or saved? She couldn't decide. "Then you'd better get it."

"Wait." Liam stopped her retreat to the other side of the bed with a hand on her arm.

She turned back to face him and he gave her a quick kiss. The mattress bounced a little as he got up. She got a good look at his broad back and fine butt encased in black cotton boxer briefs as he hurried into the living area.

Grabbing her robe and pulling it on, she followed him into the other room.

"Hey, Dad. What's up?" He listened and winced. "I should have known this would happen. We had planned to tell you when you got back. So we could do it in person."

Ellie couldn't hear the other end of the conversation but she imagined Mac being more hurt than angry if he'd heard the news from someone else.

Liam rolled his eyes when their gazes met and she smiled.

"Yeah, you did and I was but—" Liam nodded. "I will and yes, I was with her when we told her parents. Thanks. Talk to you soon."

He placed the phone back on the counter. Blowing out his breath, he rubbed a hand over his face.

"I take it your dad found out?"

He nodded and rubbed a hand across his face.

"Meg?"

"Fiona. Dad said at first he thought she was talking about Meg's pregnancy but Fiona clarified before Meg could get the phone away from her."

"Was he angry?" She felt bad that Mac had found out through someone else, but at least it was a family member.

Liam rubbed the back of his neck. "Not about us

not telling him. He understood the situation with them being out of town."

Yeah, Mac was a pretty reasonable guy. "Let me guess, he doesn't understand the friends-having-a-baby part."

Liam stabbed a finger in the air. "That would be the one."

She put her arms around his waist and gave him a loose hug. "Once the baby is here, he'll be thrilled."

"Yeah, I could hear Doris in the background saying congratulations." He hooked his arm around her waist, pulling her closer and kissing the top of her head.

His phone rang again. He dropped his arm and stepped away. "And that'll be my sister."

He picked up the phone and pointed the screen at her. "Told ya."

"Uh-oh." Ellie laughed.

Liam swiped his thumb and answered. "Well, if it isn't my blabbermouth sister."

Ellie was close enough to hear Meg apologizing on the other end.

"When has Fiona ever been able to keep a secret? She takes after someone else I know." He quirked a smile. "Yeah, you. As I've said before, it's like growing up with you all over again."

While he was talking with Meg, she pulled out ingredients to make breakfast. Most mornings she ate cereal but the thought didn't appeal, and since Liam was here, she decided on scrambled eggs and sausages.

Liam set his phone back down. "Do I have time for a quick shower before breakfast?"

"Sure."

After breakfast, he helped her clean up the kitchen.

"I noticed your tire pressure light was on so I thought I'd take your car to get some air in the tires and fill you up your gas tank."

"Okay." She found her purse and pulled out her wallet to reimburse him.

"Ellie." He shook his head. "Put that away."

"But…"

"No buts." He leaned over and kissed her forehead. "We're in this together."

Ellie stayed home to catch up on some studying for an upcoming exam. She wasn't sure if she'd be able to finish her degree requirements in time for her plans for getting a job at the proposed assisted living and nursing facility, but she still needed to keep up with the classes she was taking.

The money she'd been spending on school might be better spent on a bigger apartment. This one would be crowded with a baby. *There's always Liam's offer of one of his rentals*, an inner voice reminded her.

She frowned and rubbed her stomach, sending a silent apology to the new life growing inside. Was being stubborn going to mean her baby would ultimately suffer for her decisions? Or would getting involved with someone who coped with emotions by pulling away and burying himself in work be worse?

The apartment door opened and she slammed her book shut, realizing she hadn't really studied. "That took a while."

Liam closed the door behind him. "I got your oil changed, too."

"You didn't have to do that."

"Ogle insisted. Said it was time." Liam shrugged. "Who am I to argue?"

"Well, if Ogle wanted to do it."

"He's got some kid working for him that he said needed the experience."

"A kid? You and Ogle let a kid change my oil?" She frowned. Her tone carried a bit of annoyance, but she was touched by his actions on her behalf. It was the type of thing her dad did for her mom, even after the breakdown of their relationship; she suspected Mac had done it for Liam's mom and now for Doris. Ellie realized it was nice to have someone who had your back.

"Yeah, Kevin says hi." Liam chuckled and held up his hands in a self-protection stance.

She made a moue with her lips. "You shouldn't tease me when I'm hungry."

"Oh, no, do I have a hangry diva on my hands?" He put his arm around her shoulders and squeezed.

"Yes, you do. I slathered peanut butter on a banana for lunch, but it's worn off."

"Don't worry about it. I'm taking you out for…" Liam said and grinned. "An early supper."

"You are?" Her heart skipped a beat. *As in a date?* Here they were, having a baby and never actually been on a real date. That strange quasi-date at Hennen's when they'd run into Mike and Colton didn't count.

"I'm here, so we may as well hang out together."

Oh, but she yearned for more than hanging out. She wanted them to be a couple—a family—a real family. Maybe she should come right out and tell him what she wanted. How could you get something if you didn't ask for it? "Liam, I—"

"Maybe if we'd gone out more, we might not be in this situation," he interrupted.

Maybe now wasn't the time for confessions. She managed a little laugh. "You think?"

His blue eyes twinkled as he regarded her. "Nah, not really. I think it's payback from the universe for all the comments I make about Meg and Riley."

"I think it was a little more than that."

"Really?" He raised his eyebrows. "Maybe you need to show me…just so I'll know better in the future."

"Nice try, but you promised to take me out to supper and I'm starving." Not that she didn't want to explore that chemistry again, but hunger took precedence.

He sighed. "If I feed you, maybe we can revisit this discussion?"

She tilted her head from side to side as if sizing him up. "Perhaps."

"There's nothing more appealing than a decisive woman." He draped an arm around her shoulders and laughed. "So, when you're not tossing your cookies, you're hungry. Have I got that right?"

"It's not funny. Sometimes I feel as though I'm all over the map. One minute happy, the next crying. And food I used to love makes me sick just to think about it."

"I hate to disagree…especially with a pregnant woman but…" He gently rubbed his knuckles across the top of her head. "It's a bit funny from where I'm standing, but I will take you out to eat."

"Ha, you weren't exactly Mr. Calm-and-Collected when I was losing it in your bathroom."

He sighed. "You had me scared to death."

She knew he was probably thinking of his mother, so she didn't tease. "Sorry."

He gave her a smile that melted her heart. "Let's get some food in you before you become unbearable."

Scooting out from under his arm—even though it felt heavenly—she said, "Sounds like a plan."

He reached behind him and scooped up her car keys from the kitchen counter. "Ready?"

"You're driving?"

He jangled her keys and tilted his head. "No?"

"Fine, but quit messing with the presets on my radio."

"If you had decent music, I wouldn't be forced to listen to the radio." He shook his head, looking at her as if he pitied her.

She pushed him toward the door. "We won't listen to anything then. I'll serenade you."

"Oh, good Lord." He stopped dead in his tracks.

She plowed into him and swatted his freaking broad shoulders. "Hey!"

He chuckled and captured her hand and threaded his fingers through hers. "C'mon, let's go."

Chapter Twelve

Ellie hummed to herself the next morning as she pulled out a carton of eggs from the refrigerator. Liam had gotten out of bed and brought her saltine crackers to settle her stomach before jumping into the shower.

Having breakfast ready for him was a good way to repay the favor. She was dicing peppers and onions when her cell phone rang. She wiped her hands on the kitchen towel hanging over the oven handle before answering.

"Ellie, so glad I caught you." Meg sounded a little breathless.

"What's up?" Ellie frowned.

"I really hate to bother you on your day off, but do you think you could watch James for a couple hours today? Riley got called in to work and I'd already promised to help chaperone Fiona's class trip to the pumpkin patch."

"Sure." Ellie glanced at the clock on the stove. "Do I have time to shower and get dressed?"

"Of course. Thanks, I really appreciate this."

"No problem. I'll be there as soon as I can."

Liam appeared in the in the living area, his jeans unbuttoned and riding low on his hips, the band from his boxer briefs visible. He was shirtless, a towel thrown over his shoulder. "Did you get called in to work or something?"

"No. That was Meg. She asked if I could help her out." She swallowed as her gaze took in his gloriously bare chest, remembering how those muscles reacted to her touch.

"What does Meg need help with?"

Of course if he was on one of those calendars, then all women would be drooling over the six-pack abs and the dusting of hair that formed a V and disappeared under the waistband of his jeans. His dark hair was more disheveled than normal.

"Ellie? My sister?"

She forced her gaze upward and her thoughts on the conversation, but it wasn't easy. Liam wasn't musclebound like a weight lifter, but he was fit. Oh, boy, was he ever.

Clearing her throat, she explained, "Meg asked if I could watch James while she helps chaperone Fiona's class trip to the pumpkin patch."

He tossed the towel over the back of the chair and picked up a gray waffle-weave henley draped over the back of the couch. "What time does she need you?"

"As soon as I shower and dress." She checked her watch.

"Do you want some breakfast before we head over?" he said and pulled the shirt over his head.

Her heart rate kicked up. "Oh, you're coming with me?"

"Is that okay with you?" He grabbed his sneakers and sat on the sofa.

"Sure. I had already started on breakfast but I'd better jump in the shower instead."

He stuffed his feet into his sneakers. "What were you making?"

"The ingredients for omelets are on the counter."

He finished tying his laces and came to stand next to her. "Go get in the shower. I can handle omelets."

Liam drank a quick cup of coffee while Ellie was in the shower and rinsed the cup in the sink. He finished chopping the peppers and onions and set about making omelets. He was putting the plates on the breakfast bar when she came back from her shower. They ate quickly and Liam stacked the plates in the sink before they left.

Meg met them at the door, holding James on her hip, the dog at her side. The baby had a piece of a banana clutched in his fist. "Ooh, two for the price of one."

Liam bumped shoulders with Ellie. "You didn't say you were getting paid. Trying to get out of sharing with me?"

Meg led them through the small original living room into the new, expansive family room with large windows and patio doors looking into the woods at the back of the house. They didn't have a deck or patio yet, but Riley hoped to put one in soon.

"Yeah, good luck getting to those snickerdoodles before me," Ellie said, and smiled at James and gave him a kiss on the top of his head. "Hello there, little man."

He waved the banana around and showed her a toothy grin. The dog, an Aussiedoodle with reddish-brown curls, whined, his intent gaze on the fruit.

Meg wiped a piece of banana off his cheek. "He was just finishing his morning snack. I haven't had a chance to get him washed yet."

The baby thrust the smashed banana toward Liam. "Meem."

"Thanks, buddy, but I just ate."

"I can get him cleaned up." Ellie reached out and took James in her arms. "Looks like you're enjoying that nanner, bud."

Meg nodded. "Bananas are his new favorite snack."

He offered it to Ellie, but she shook her head, her lips clamped firmly together. James, imitating her by vigorously shaking his head, opened his fist and let the banana piece fall, but Mangy scooped it up in midair.

Meg laughed. "You guys might want to consider getting a dog."

Remembering how upset Ellie had gotten over the thought of taking care of a pet, Liam winced. He glared at his sister, shaking his head, but Meg threw him a puzzled look. His gaze went to Ellie, but evidently she was too busy talking to James to be upset.

Meg kissed James before Ellie took him to wash his hands and face. She turned to Liam. "What was that all about? Ellie likes dogs. So do you."

He swiped a hand over his face. "It's a long story."

"And I'm in a hurry. Any questions before I leave?"

Liam glanced at the flat screen he and Riley had

mounted to the wall. "As a matter of fact I do. Tell me again the channel number for ESPN on your television."

"I don't know." Meg picked up her purse and keys.

"How can you not know something that important?"

"Yeah, like I have time to watch television. By the time I get Fiona and James down for the night, I'm ready to crawl into bed myself, especially with Riley on nights." Meg patted her still-flat stomach. "At least by the time this one comes, he'll have enough seniority to get a day shift when one becomes available."

"Okay. Jeez. Sorry I asked." He threw up his hands in a defensive gesture but laughed when Meg held up a fist. "I'm sure I can find it."

Meg lowered her arm. "You'll have to find the remote first. It's James's new favorite thing now that he can lift up against the coffee table."

"Not exactly running a tight ship, are we, sis?" As soon as he said it, he realized his mistake. Meg would have plenty of opportunities to point out parenting errors to him in the near future.

She gave him a big, evil smile. "Oh, I am so going to enjoy picking on you when you have one running around."

"Ellie and I will have it all under control." *Nothing like compounding your mistakes.*

"Ha! I love it." Meg laughed and rubbed her palms together. "You are so clueless. I'd help you look for the remote, but I'm already running late."

"So much for sitting around watching sports highlights in my underwear," he muttered as he lifted couch cushions in his search for the remote. Each time he lifted a cushion Mangy stuck his shaggy head under it. He patted the dog's head as he pushed it out of the way so he could replace the cushion. "What you looking for, boy?"

The dog whined and stuck his nose in the space between the arm and the cushion, grabbing something.

Liam latched onto the dog's collar before he could scamper off with his treasure. He pried a set of plastic keys from the animal's mouth.

"What are you two doing?" Ellie stood in the doorway to the large family room, James perched on her hip. The baby spotted the dog and grunted and lunged, but Ellie managed to hang on.

"Mangy and I were looking for the remote and he found these." The dog sat and whined as his gaze followed Liam's hand. "Sorry, boy, I doubt these are yours."

"Here, you take James and I'll wash those keys off."

He shook his head. "If I set them down, the dog is going to run off with them."

She leaned down and put James on the floor. "You stay here with Uncle Meem while I take care of this."

"Don't start with that Meem stuff. I just got Fiona to say it correctly."

"Meem… Meem… Meem," James babbled as he crawled to the coffee table and pulled himself up. One hand rested on the table and the other stretched toward Liam.

Liam tossed the keys to Ellie and reached down to ruffle his nephew's hair. "Hey, buddy, not sure what you're talking about. Can you say 'Liam'?"

"Sorry, but I think you're going to be Uncle Leem or Meem for the foreseeable future. At least you won't have to worry about that with ours."

Liam looked up from his search for the remote. "Why not?"

Ellie clicked her teeth. "Because she will be calling you Daddy."

"Oh, yeah." He scratched his scalp and frowned. "What?"

"That's a scary thought, but I guess if my baby sister and Riley can do it, so can we." Had his dad gotten a mini panic attack thinking about being a parent before Liam was born?

"Can we?"

"You certainly can, you're an ER nurse. Of course you're qualified." Ellie was going to be great. He wished he had as much confidence in himself as he did her.

"Bet they wouldn't let me take home a baby if they knew how scattered I've been lately."

"I find that hard to believe." He jammed his fingers in the back of the couch. That damn remote had to be here somewhere.

She sank down next to James as he slapped his palm on the coffee table. "Believe it. I poured orange juice on my cornflakes last week."

"Run out of milk?" His searching fingers found something and he pulled out a tiny pink plastic hardhat. What the…?

"No, I didn't run out of milk. I pulled out the OJ by mistake."

"What did you do?" He started to set the tiny toy on the coffee table but looked at James and decided against it.

"I threw them out and started over, but what's that got to do with it?"

"It proves you're good at problem solving, because I would have eaten them."

"You are such a guy."

He wiggled his eyebrows. "Glad you finally noticed. Aha, here's the remote."

Ellie rolled her eyes. "Give that hat to me and I'll put it in Fiona's room. It belongs to her Barbie Builder set."

"How do you know these things?" He put the cushions back on the sofa.

"It's a girl thing."

"Hey, James, how about we watch some sports? Make sure that father of yours is teaching you the right teams to root for." He scooped his nephew off the floor and sat down on the sofa with him.

"I think he's wet. Let me go get a fresh diaper."

Liam held James up in the air. "Now she tells me. Are you wet?"

The boy let out a string of baby giggles.

Ellie came back with a diaper and tub of wipes. "Want me to take him?"

"It's okay. I've changed Fiona's. May as well get some more practice in." He truly did want to be involved.

He put James on the blanket on the floor and unsnapped the baby's pants to get at the diaper. At least he remembered how to do that much from when Fiona was a baby. He removed the soggy diaper.

"Liam, wait! Put this over…"

He glanced up as Ellie launched what looked like a washcloth at him.

What the heck was she on about? He knew how to— Something wet and warm squirted all over the front of his shirt.

He glanced down at his giggling nephew. "Why did he do that?"

Ellie had her fist pressed against her mouth and her shoulders were shaking. She cleared her throat. "It's something baby boys do."

"Why didn't you warn me?" After getting over being grossed out, he could appreciate the humor in it. And he couldn't be angry with an innocent—he glanced down at his giggling nephew. Huh, maybe not quite so innocent.

"I thought you knew. You said you'd changed diapers before," Ellie said.

"I changed Fiona's diaper a time or two and nothing like this ever happened." He shook his head.

"Girls are different but it can still happen."

"So, is there a trick to not getting wet?"

"I think the trick is to keep something over him like the old diaper or a cloth."

"Why would I know something like this?"

"You've never changed James's diaper before?" He shook his head and she continued, "Well, now you know. Look on the bright side, at least your face wasn't in the line of fire."

James began laughing and Liam put his palm over the baby's belly and tickled him. "You think that's funny? Now I'm going to have to wear one of your daddy's shirts and I'll make your mommy wash mine."

The baby giggled. "Meem."

He shook his head at James. There was so much he didn't know about babies and kids despite having spent a lot of time around his niece and nephew. Had his dad been nervous and clueless in the beginning? Maybe by the time his child was old enough to form memories of his or her childhood, he'd have a better handle on the whole parenting thing.

* * *

Once again, Ellie awoke to a cold, empty bed. She'd been doing that ever since Liam's friend Nick had picked him up three days earlier. She rolled over and rubbed her hand over the cool sheets. Liam had only slept over for a few nights, but she'd gotten used to having him here.

She had no idea when she'd see him again. He'd told her that during his time off he was taking an extra shift at one of the part-time stations. He apologized and explained that this had been planned for a while.

Sighing, she got up and pulled on her pink fleece robe against the apartment's early-morning chill. She paused to see if this was a morning sickness day. It wasn't. At least not yet. Of course her nausea didn't just strike first thing; sometimes it lasted all day or hit unexpectedly. Smells could trigger it, too.

The nausea had been getting worse but she knew the extra hormones that caused it kicked in around the eight-week mark, so it wasn't surprising.

Today was her first appointment with the obstetrician. She'd be going alone and part of that was her fault. She'd assured Liam that the checkup was just routine and it was, but now that she was faced with going alone, it felt…sad. It was still early in the pregnancy for the doctor to want an ultrasound. At least Liam wasn't missing out on something like that.

Buck up, Ellie, and quit your whining.

Liam had stepped up, but the fact that they lived three hours apart wasn't going to change unless she moved to Boston. Pulling up stakes, leaving everything she knew and had worked for to move so she could live on the periphery of Liam's life, held no appeal.

"But I'm reserving the right to revisit this decision," she told her reflection as she brushed her hair before dashing out the door.

At the doctor's office, Ellie flipped through old magazines, kicking herself for not remembering to bring a book. Not that it mattered since she doubted she'd be able to concentrate any better on the latest spy thriller than she could this three-month-old *People* magazine. Too many things running through her head. Being in the medical profession at times like this was not helpful.

The blood tests scheduled for today might be routine, but this was *her* baby they were running tests on. That changed everything. She was doing this so she could be prepared, not because she suspected something was wrong. Intellectually she knew her chances of a successful pregnancy were the same as anyone else's, but emotions didn't always operate on facts. But the situation gave her some perspective on what her parents must've gone through when her cancer was diagnosed.

Would she be faced one day with her child having a life-threatening illness? Her hand covered her still flat stomach as sympathy for her parents filled her.

She glanced around the waiting room at the other women in various stages of pregnancy, some with partners, others alone like her.

Heaving a sigh, she tossed the magazine aside just as the inner door opened and the nurse called her name.

Ellie jumped up. At least doing something would be better than just sitting and waiting.

The nurse smiled. "Ellie, it's so good to see you again."

Ellie recognized the woman from hospital rotations during nursing school. "Kim Smith, right?"

"It's Dawson now." The nurse led her down a hallway.

"Mine's still Harding, but I guess you could see that from the chart." Ellie hated the warmth in her cheeks. Plenty of single women had babies these days. Even in Loon Lake.

"It's been a while." Kim stopped in front of a balance beam scale. "How have you been?"

"Is that a professional question or making conversation?"

"Both, I guess." Kim laughed. "Okay, hop up on the scale."

"I hate this part." Ellie sighed and glanced at her red sneakers. "Can I take these off first?"

"Really? At your first appointment." Kim clicked her tongue but grinned. "This is only the beginning."

Ellie glanced at her feet and debated, but giggled and toed her shoes off.

Kim marked her weight on the chart. "Okay, take a seat and we'll get blood pressure next."

"You should've done that *before* you weighed me." Ellie motioned toward the scale. "Having to get on that thing probably raised it."

Kim chuckled. "So you're feeling okay? No complaints?"

"I'm doing good, if you don't count the morning sickness that pops up at all hours and crying over the stupidest things." Ellie sat in the chair and rolled up her sleeve.

"I hear that. I carried sandwich bags and tissues in my purse." Kim set the chart on the table. "Take a seat and we'll get your pressure, then some labs, but I guess you know the drill."

Ellie nodded. "Yeah, I know all this stuff like getting a patient's blood pressure is standard procedure, but when it's being done to you, it doesn't feel routine at all."

So far there was no need for Liam to be here for these mundane things. So why did she feel so bereft?

"Yeah, we don't always make the best patients, do we?" Kim adjusted the blood pressure cuff on her upper left arm. "You still like working in the ER?"

"I do, but I've been thinking of a change." Ellie laid her other hand over her stomach. "Especially now. Do you like this kind of nursing?"

"I'm sure it's not as exciting or interesting as the ER but the hours are easier. Plus, holidays and weekends off is nice for family life." Kim made notes on the chart as the Dinamap displayed her blood pressure.

Ellie nodded. From now on, she'd have someone else to take into consideration. Working twelve-hour shifts might not be feasible. She put out her arm but cringed when Kim came at her with the needle. Being a nurse didn't make getting stuck any easier.

"We should have the results back in one to two weeks." Kim marked the vials of blood. "And we'll just take a quick look today to verify the pregnancy and check for iron and vitamin levels. We'll need to get you started on prenatal vitamins."

After a week of denying her suspicions, Ellie had decided she needed to be proactive. "Yeah, I took some over-the-counter ones, but they don't have the same folic acid levels."

"I've got everything I need. It was good seeing you again." Kim opened the door and dropped the chart in the holder on the door. "The doctor should be in shortly."

Ten minutes felt like an eternity and Ellie was starting to get antsy when the door opened and Kim popped her head in. "The doctor has decided he'd like you to have an ultrasound. Fortunately, we can do one on-site. The tech will be in in just a minute to escort you back there."

Ellie's stomach twisted into knots. Not since being diagnosed with cancer had she felt so helpless. "Tell me what's wrong. Why do they want to do an ultrasound now? What can't wait?"

"Ellie, you of all people know I can't say anything." Kim shook her head. "Let's keep the imagination reined in," she added with a smile before closing the door.

Ellie glared at the closed door Kim had escaped through and wrung her hands. Was she overreacting? The way she saw it, she was allowed to do so. This was *her* baby, maybe her only chance to be a mom.

She should have said yes when her mother had offered to come. But she would've had to take off work and Ellie hated for her to use her PTO to come to a routine first exam. She had assumed the most exciting part would be to hear the baby's heartbeat. Except being alone with only her thoughts for company wasn't a good idea. She sat on her hands trying to keep them warm and swung her legs.

There was a quick rap on the door.

"Finally," she muttered. At least they'd be getting this show on the road. Despite Kim's advice, she'd let her imagination run roughshod over her rational self.

The door opened but instead of the ultrasound tech or the doctor, the receptionist stood in the doorway. "Someone is insisting on seeing you, but we can't let anyone back here without your permission."

Had her mother come, anyway? Who else could it

be? The receptionist cleared her throat and Ellie nodded. "Yes, that's fine."

Before she could react, Liam loomed in the doorway, still in his dark blue BFD uniform. She blinked, but he didn't disappear. Liam was here! Oh, God, the news was so bad they called him. No wait, that was crazy. They hadn't done anything yet and he couldn't have gotten here in such a short time even if he'd been in town. Nothing had been wrong ten minutes ago… but was it now?

Chapter Thirteen

She straightened and pulled her hands from under her thighs. "What are you doing here? How did you get here? How did you find me?"

He shut the door and crossed the small room in two strides. "I'm here because I was serious when I said wanted to be involved. I hit the road as soon as I got off shift this morning and I called Meg to ask where you'd be," he said, ticking off his answers by holding up his fingers. "I think that covers all your questions."

"You don't know how glad I am to see you." Ellie swallowed several times, trying to keep it together, fiercely holding back the tears burning at the back of her eyes. "Something isn't right."

He stood directly in front of her, then nudged himself between her legs until his thighs rested against the table. "What is it? What's wrong?"

"I don't know. It was supposed to be just a routine exam and labs but then…then…" She waved her hands in front of her, fumbling for words.

Without a word, he pulled her into the shelter of his arms and held her close. *She loved him.* She was in love with Liam. Not a schoolgirl crush. Not lust for a sexy-as-sin fireman. But soul-deep, forever love.

She snuffled against his chest. "Oh, Liam, what if something's wrong with our baby?"

His arms tightened into a bear hug. "Then we'll deal with it."

"Did…" He cleared his throat and loosened his hold. "Did they say what could be wrong?"

She shook her head and eased away from him enough so she could speak. "No, but they test for Down syndrome. But they won't have those results for at least a week. I don't know what this means."

He rubbed her back. "The receptionist didn't act like anything was wrong."

"She probably doesn't know and even if she did, they're not allowed to say anything." Next time she was faced with an angry relative demanding answers, she'd have a lot more sympathy.

"Ellie?" Kim opened the door. Her eyes widened when she spotted Liam, her gaze taking in his uniform. "Oh, I didn't know anyone had come with you."

Liam stepped away from Ellie and held out his hand. "Liam McBride. I arrived a bit late. I came after getting off shift this morning."

"Off shift?" She glanced at the Boston patch on his shirt and lifted an eyebrow. "As in Boston off shift?"

Liam nodded. "That's the one."

Ellie leaned to the side so she could see around Liam. "Liam's the…uh, baby daddy."

What a silly thing to call him, but it was the easiest explanation.

"Nice meeting you, Liam. I'm Kim. Ellie and I went through nursing school at the same time." Kim shook his hand. "They've got the ultrasound ready for you. It's just down the hall. Ellie, you can leave your things in here."

Kim glanced at Liam. "Umm…if you'll—"

"I want him with me," Ellie said, and reached for his hand.

Kim nodded. "Of course, I just thought he might want to wait here while we get you ready."

Liam paced the small room, waiting for the nurse to come and get him. His gut churned with every step. Was something wrong with Ellie? Or the baby?

Every time the word *cancer* tried to invade his brain, he shoved it aside and slammed the door. *One worry at a time, McBride.*

"Wait until they tell us," he muttered, and glared at the closed door.

He wanted to fling it open and demand they tell them something. He wanted to run to Ellie and hold her and make everything okay.

Thank goodness he'd listened to his gut, not to mention his conscience, when it told him he should be with Ellie. She had needed him. How could he have thought she didn't? Her assertion that it was just a routine exam had rung false because this was *their* baby. Nothing would be just routine for either of them. But this…

He couldn't imagine leaving her to go through this

uncertainty alone. He remembered his promise to be strong when she needed him to be. It looked like it would be his turn to be the strong one today.

The door opened and he resisted the urge to pounce on Kim and demand answers.

"We're ready for you," she announced cheerfully.

He followed the nurse to a room with complicated-looking equipment and a monitor on a rolling stand. Ellie lay on her back on an exam table with her knees up and a sheet draped over the bottom half of her body.

"This is Liam," Kim said to a technician.

The technician looked up. "Hi; I'm Sherrie."

"I'll leave you to it," Kim said. "Sherrie will take good care of you."

Sherrie smiled as she got her equipment ready. "You know we won't be able to determine the baby's sex yet."

"Yeah, that's not why we're here," Ellie told her.

The other woman nodded. "I wanted to get that out of the way so you won't be disappointed."

Liam went to stand next to Ellie and she reached for his hand.

The technician got out what looked like a wand and rolled a rubber sheath on it. Ellie squeezed his hand. He winked at her and she grinned, some of the tension melting away. He leaned close to her ear.

"I think it's a little too late to give me pointers now," he whispered.

She choked on a laugh.

"Okay, if you could relax for me now, Ellie," the technician said, and scooted the stool to the end of the exam table.

He laced his fingers through Ellie's and pulled her hand against his chest. Watching the monitor, he tried to make sense of what he was seeing. The technician's face gave nothing away. He'd bet they were trained to not reveal anything.

"I'm just going to call the doctor in." Sherrie stood and scooted out the door.

"Liam?" Ellie looked from the closed door and back to him. "I thought I saw—but her face was blank."

"Hey, hey, calm down." Brushing the hair back from her cheek, he tucked it behind her ear and cupped his palm against her jaw. He pressed his lips against her forehead. "You know yourself, technicians aren't allowed to tell you anything."

"They tell you good stuff like 'Oh, look, there's your perfectly healthy baby.'" Ellie sniffed. "If she went to get the doctor, that means something is wrong. Oh, Liam, I'm scared."

"Look at me." He leaned over so his face was directly in front of hers. "Whatever it is, we'll handle it together. I'm not going anywhere."

Tough talk from a guy who'd rather be feeling his way through thick smoke in an unfamiliar structure in danger of collapsing than to be here right now. Ellie's fear gutted him and his belly clenched.

A man with a thick thatch of gray hair hustled in and introduced himself. Liam shook hands but he couldn't hear the man's name above the roaring in his ears.

"Let's take a look and see what we have." Dr. Stanley put on a pair of glasses and settled on a stool in front of the screen.

"What is it?" Ellie asked in a hoarse voice.

The doctor slid his glasses onto the top of his head. "It appears there are two embryos."

Liam cleared his throat. "T-two?"

Dr. Stanley nodded. "Congratulations. You're having twins."

The man's words caused all the air to swoosh out of Liam's lungs. Wait…what? Twins? Was that even possible? *Of course it's possible, dumbass.*

"Thank you… I don't know what to say. I'm so relieved. Thank you," Ellie was saying to Dr. What's-His-Name. "Isn't wonderful, Liam? Liam?"

The doctor jumped up and pushed the rolling stool toward Liam. "Son, I think you need this more than I do."

Liam sank down, still trying to digest the information. Of course he was ecstatic that nothing was wrong…but two babies? At the same time? "You're sure?"

"Most definitely. It's too early to determine the sex yet, but I can tell you they're fraternal." The doctor slipped his glasses back down onto his nose to look at the monitor again. "Everything looks normal for twins. Of course with multiples, we'll want to monitor you a bit more closely, especially toward the end, but I see no reason for concern."

"With fraternal, we could have one of each," Ellie said. "Meg will claim we're trying to keep up with her."

Dr. Stanley glanced between them. "Well, if you don't have any questions, I'll have Kim give you some pamphlets on multiples and a prescription for prenatal vitamins."

"Thank you, Doctor, I'm just relieved everything is okay," Ellie said.

"Sorry if you had some anxious moments, but rest assured, everything appears normal." With a quick nod of his head, he stuck out his hand to Liam. "Congratulations again, son."

Liam shook hands with the other man, but if asked to describe him after he left the room, he wouldn't have a clue. It was as if he was experiencing the world through his respirator…his breathing loud in his ears while everything else was muffled.

"You look a little shell-shocked," Kim observed as she led him to the previous exam room while Ellie got cleaned up and dressed.

"I was just wrapping my head around one and now it's two…at once." His voice cracked on the last part.

Kim patted him on the shoulder. "Believe me, this isn't the first time I've seen that look. Before you leave, I'll put you in touch with the local support group for multiples."

"Support group for multiples…" Liam shook his head. "That's a thing?"

She chuckled. "Yup. Your reaction to the news is quite typical."

"Ellie should be back in a moment," Kim added and left.

He needed to hold it together for Ellie. Today's news was unexpected but he could handle it and keep everything under control. Sitting hunched forward with his elbows on his thighs, his mind raced at the thought of two babies. Would having twins put more of a strain on Ellie's body? Having her move to Boston seemed even more urgent now, but he knew better than to confront her. Ellie could be stubborn. He stared at his boots as if they could supply him with answers. Maybe he'd talk to Meg. This was a role reversal…asking his little sister for advice.

* * *

Standing next to Liam on Meg and Riley's porch, Ellie knocked on the door. Meg had insisted they come to supper while Liam was in Loon Lake. Ellie wasn't quite sure how she felt about Meg treating them as a couple. It wouldn't be long before the whole town was doing that, especially with Liam showing up in time for the ultrasound. The medical personnel couldn't say anything but that privacy didn't extend to the people in the waiting room. Liam showing up in his uniform hadn't gone unnoticed.

Waiting for Meg or Riley to answer, Ellie turned to Liam. "This feels like déjà vu."

He wiggled his eyebrows. "Yup. Déjà vu all over again."

She rolled her eyes but was glad he could joke. His face had drained of color when the doctor had told them she was expecting twins. He'd recovered quickly, but she could see he'd been putting on a happy face. Once the relief that nothing was wrong passed, the truth of her situation had started to sink in. She was going to be a single mother to twins. She wiped her clammy hands on the front of her jeans. Her initial relief that nothing was wrong had started to wear off and it was sinking in that the situation she thought she'd had under control this morning had done a one-eighty.

The door swung open and Riley greeted them with a sobbing James in his arms. "C'mon in. Sorry about this."

"Oh, no. What's wrong?" Ellie's heart ached for a now-hiccuping James. And for herself. She was going to have this, times two!

"He's crying because he's not allowed to play with Fiona's toys." Riley stood aside so they could enter.

"Worried about his masculinity?" Liam chuckled as he stepped into the living room.

Meg appeared and clucked her tongue at her brother. "It's a choking hazard. All those little pieces go in his mouth."

Liam glanced around. "Where is Fiona?"

"She had a half day of school and she went out to Brody and Mary's farm. She spent the afternoon entertaining Elliott so Mary could catch up on some paperwork. They'll bring her home later tonight."

James threw his arms toward Meg. "Mommy."

Riley ruffled his son's hair before handing him over to Meg. Turning his attention to his guests, he motioned with his head. "C'mon in and sit, you two. Supper isn't ready yet. We got a little behind with all the ruckus."

Ellie draped her jacket over the back of the sofa. "Can I help with anything?"

"Thanks, but I have it under control...for the moment." Meg laughed and tickled James's tummy and the baby burst into giggles. "But Riley can take my brother with him to help get the grill ready."

"Maybe we should give them our news first," Ellie said, and glanced at Liam.

Meg looked from one to the other. "More news? Does this mean you two are—"

"The news was from the doctor," Ellie interrupted. She didn't want Meg getting the wrong idea and starting a discussion she had no intention of engaging in.

"Is there something wrong?" Meg adjusted James on her hip. "Guys, you're scaring me."

"No, it's okay." Ellie put a hand over her stomach. "They said the babies are fine."

"Oh, well that's— Wait! Did you say *babies*? As in plural?" Eyes wide, Meg pointed to Ellie's stomach. "You mean…"

"Twins." Ellie couldn't help grinning. She was still riding high, grateful that nothing was wrong. At one point in her life she hadn't been sure she'd be able to have kids at all because of the cancer treatments. At the time of her treatment, being able to get pregnant didn't mean a whole lot but as she got older, having a baby became more important. Now to have two, while daunting, was a real blessing.

Meg shifted James and gave Ellie a one-armed hug. "I'm so happy for you. I know… Well, I just want you to know how happy I am."

When Meg pulled away, Riley gave Ellie a hug. "Congratulations."

"And you, too, bro." Meg gave Liam a quick hug. "Leave it to Liam to try to outdo me."

"I told you she would say that!" Liam scowled at his sister.

Meg sniffed and stuck her nose in the air. "Of course you'd have to be having triplets to catch up, or quad—"

"Bite your tongue," Liam grumbled.

Ellie raised her hand and waved it about. "Let's not forget I'm the one carrying these babies."

"Sorry." Meg laughed. "I'll settle for being an auntie twice over."

"Are there any twins in either of your families?" Riley asked.

"None that we know of. I asked my mom when I called to tell her the news," Ellie said.

"I'll bet she's excited," Meg said.

Ellie nodded. "She's already trying to decide what she wants to be called."

Meg laughed. "She may not get a choice. Fiona called Doris 'Mrs. Grampa Mac' for the longest time."

James pointed a finger at Liam. "Meem."

Everyone laughed and James bounced on Meg's hip, as if proud of having made everyone laugh.

Ellie's throat closed up and threatened to choke her. If, in the future, she and Liam weren't a couple, would he bring the children to McBride family gatherings without her? Would her kids come home and tell her how much fun they'd had? She blinked against the sudden burning in her eyes.

"Yeah, your kids seem to have a problem with names," Liam said, but the look he gave James made Ellie's insides feel all squishy. He might not believe it yet, but he was going to make a great dad.

"And I suppose yours won't?" Meg shot back. "You can call him anything you want, sweetie," she told James in a stage whisper. "Maybe when you get older, I can teach you a few other names."

Riley chuckled and clapped a hand over Liam's shoulder. "Maybe you'd better come help me get the steaks on the grill before you dig yourself an even deeper hole."

With the guys outside, Ellie helped Meg get James ready for bed.

"Pretty soon, we'll be doing this together to your kids," Meg remarked as she put pajamas on James.

"I have a feeling I'll be coming to you a lot for advice," Ellie told her.

Meg picked up her sleepy son and cuddled him. "I'll be here for you. You know that, right?"

"Of course, and I know Liam's going to be a great dad." And she did believe it.

"He will," Meg agreed, and gave James a small blanket with satin binding.

"Nigh-nigh." James hugged the ragged blanket to him and stuck his thumb in his mouth.

"Is it always this easy to get him to bed?"

Meg shook her head as she laid him in his crib. "I wish. No, he calls the security blanket his 'night-night.' I put him in his crib a few times when he was actually asking for his blanket."

Ellie went with Meg back to the kitchen to get the rest of the supper ready while the guys finished grilling the steaks.

Ellie was setting the bottles of salad dressing on the table when Liam came back in carrying a plate of foil-wrapped baked potatoes, Riley was behind him carrying a platter of grilled steaks.

"Hope you ladies are hungry," Riley said as he set the platter on the table.

Meg stepped behind Riley and put her arms around his waist. "For you, dear, always."

Liam made gagging sounds. "How are we supposed to eat now?"

"Can't you control him?" Meg asked Ellie.

Ellie shrugged it off with a grin, but her stomach clenched because she longed for what Meg had with Riley. Liam's pallor over having twins was fresh in her mind, along with the way he'd been fake-smiling on the porch. She needed a relationship that could withstand whatever life threw at them. Was that asking too much?

With a scrape of chairs, they all sat down and began dishing out the food.

"Will you be staying in your current apartment once the babies are born?" Meg asked as she passed the bowl of salad.

Ellie was hyperaware of Liam next to her. "For now. But twins changes things a bit. I had thought I could squeeze a crib into my place...but two?"

She was aware of him tensing and she rushed on, "I definitely want to look for a place in Loon Lake. Staying here is important to me."

In her peripheral vision she saw Liam press his lips together but didn't say anything.

Meg snagged a steak and put it on her plate. "Wouldn't it be awesome if you could buy that house next door?"

"But the property isn't for sale," Riley pointed out as he passed the platter of potatoes.

Meg nodded. "I know, but the owner has had trouble keeping it consistently rented. I'm not sure why."

"That's easy," Liam said. "It's because they have to live next to you, sister dear."

Meg pulled a face. "If you think you're safe because you're on the other side of the table, think again."

"Riley, have you no control over your wife?" Liam joked as he opened the foil on his baked potato.

Riley leaned over and kissed his wife. "Happy wife. Happy life. Right, dear?"

"Jeez, you've got him brainwashed," Liam grumbled, but he was grinning.

"Maybe he'd be interested in a long-term rental." Ellie put butter and sour cream on her potato. "Do you have his contact information?"

"I can call the agent. I think I still have her information somewhere from when I used to clean cottages between rentals," Meg told her.

"Thanks. I'd appreciate that." Ellie knew it was a long shot, but it was worth it to get in touch with the owner. Living next to Meg and Riley would be wonderful. Her children could grow up together with their cousins, as she had.

The table fell silent while everyone started eating.

"Are you here for three days now?" Riley looked across the table at Liam.

Liam shook his head. "Nah, I have to head back tonight."

"You do? Why?" Ellie chewed on her lower lip. She'd assumed Liam would be spending his off time with her. Didn't she have a right to expect that, after the news they'd just received? It wasn't every day you found out you were going to be parents to twins. She wanted to talk about it, maybe make some plans or even argue over names, something for him to show her he was in this with her. She blinked back tears. *Hormones*, she told herself.

His gaze searched hers. "Nick worked my part-time shift today and I promised to work his tomorrow."

She met his gaze and forced a smile. "I'm so glad you could come for the appointment today, but I hate that you have to drive back tonight already."

"It's okay. It was totally worth it." He touched her arm.

"Now who is making the googly eyes." Meg *tsk*ed. "But you're forgiven because finding out you're going to be a dad twice over doesn't happen every day."

Liam's knee was bouncing up and down under the table and Ellie gently laid her hand on it. When he looked at her, she whispered, "My turn to be the calm one. Remember we said we wouldn't both freak out at the same time?"

The wink he gave her said he understood what she was doing and he put his hand over hers and squeezed, but it was as if he'd had his hand around her heart.

She blinked to clear her vision. She'd fallen in love with Liam. Sure, she hadn't had far to go, but now it was like a neon sign blinking in her head.

She swallowed, glancing around the table. What would happen to her if she moved to Boston and left behind her support system? And if she stayed in Loon Lake, could her and Liam's tenuous relationship withstand the stress of long distance? What if her cancer returned? Her heart clenched. What would happen to her children? Would another fight for her life cast a pall over this family as it had hers? Or, unlike hers, would they rally around and wrap her and the twins in their warmth?

Chapter Fourteen

Ellie rubbed her back as she left the ER after her shift. Three days had passed since she'd seen Liam and she missed him. Ever since he found out about the babies a few weeks ago, they had been spending more time together. But talking over the phone wasn't the same. She stretched her neck, trying to work out the kinks. If she was this tired and sore now, what was going to happen over the next few months? The exhaustion should ease up in the second trimester but carrying twins had to be tiring, regardless of the month. What did she have at home to make for supper? She had to eat and she had to eat right, but sometimes she was too tired to go home and do much more than make a peanut-butter-and-Marshmallow-Fluff sandwich.

She and Liam had spoken every night since he'd left. They made small talk, and every night she stopped short of admitting her love. If she said the words, put them out there, would he use them to get her to move to Boston? Would he think she said them to wrangle a proposal or him uprooting his life? She didn't know the answer so she bit her tongue and didn't say anything.

In the corridor, she looked up and saw Liam leaning against the nurses' station. Surprise had her halting mid-stride. He was chatting up the nurses, who looked enraptured by whatever story he was telling. Before she could decide if she should be jealous, he glanced over and a huge grin split his face when he spotted her. The smile, the glint in his eyes, were for her and that knowledge filled her. She felt lighter in spite of her exhaustion.

"Sorry, ladies, but it looks like my date has arrived," he said, and stepped toward her.

Ellie said goodbye to the nurses and fell into step beside Liam as they left the hospital.

"What's this about me being your date?" She asked, torn between the prospect of going out with Liam or putting her feet up in front of the television. At this time of year it was dark when she left the ER, and going home suited her.

"I was talking about feeding you," he said, and stopped under a humming sodium vapor lamp near her car.

She looked up at him in the yellowish glow from the lights. "That sounds lovely but I confess I was looking forward to going home and not moving for at least twenty-four hours."

Would he take that as a rejection? She shivered and pulled her light jacket closer around her. The temperature had dropped along with the sun.

He put his arm around her shoulders and pulled her

against his chest. "No problem. I brought things with me. We can go to your place and I'll cook while you put your feet up."

"I can't tell you how amazing that sounds." She burrowed closer to his warmth and rubbed her cheek against the soft cotton of his sweatshirt. He smelled like clean laundry.

"What were you planning on having if I hadn't shown up?" he asked, his voice rumbling in his chest.

"My old standby. A Fluffernutter," she said, referring to her craving for a peanut-butter-and-marshmallow sandwich. She pulled away enough to look up at him.

He quirked an eyebrow and his lips twitched. "On the appropriate whole-grain bread?"

"Um…" She stared at her feet.

He clicked his tongue against his teeth. "Shame on you, Ellie Harding. After all that grief you gave me."

She shrugged. "I know, but it's not the same if it's not on white bread."

"Well, if you can see your way clear to eat healthy, I brought stuff to make a stir-fry."

"That sounds wonderful. Thank you."

"Don't thank me until you taste it." He cleared his throat. "And I brought something special but you gotta eat the healthier stuff first."

"What? Are you practicing saying dad stuff?"

He laughed. "I have to start somewhere."

"About this dessert. Did you buy it or—"

He held up a finger. "I'm not saying anything except maybe a certain bakery might be involved."

She cuffed him on the shoulder. "Don't tease if you can't deliver."

"Wouldn't dream of it." He kissed the top of her head. "And believe me when I say I can deliver."

She rubbed her slightly rounded stomach. "I know you can."

"C'mon. Let's get you home so you can relax while I make supper."

"You must be tired, too, if you just came off shift."

"Yeah, but I wasn't on my feet the entire time like you and I'm not carrying around two extra people."

"But at the moment your turnout gear weighs more than these two." She pointed to her stomach.

"True, but I get to take it off at some point."

"You got me there." She laughed and rubbed her belly. "If they're wearing me out now, I can't imagine what it'll be like once they're born. I watch Mary's Elliott running around and I can't imagine two doing that at the same time."

"Just remember, you're not in this alone." He met her gaze. "You know that right?"

"Yes, I know that." She did, but part of the time he'd be nearly two hundred miles away. She didn't voice her thoughts. A lot of women had it worse. Meg had been alone until Riley returned from Afghanistan, and Mary had been a single mother with no help until she'd met Brody and they fell in love. Unlike Riley, who hadn't even known about his daughter for years, or Roger, who had rejected Mary and his son, Liam was willing to be involved. Sure, she'd vowed to live her life out loud, but there was that sticky thing called pride. Their children would tie her to Liam for a lifetime, regardless of whether or not they were a couple. If she admitted her feelings and he didn't return them, he might pity her.

She'd had enough of being pitied to last her a lifetime. It was one of those things that eroded self-esteem.

"Okay, let's get you home, warmed up and fed."

Liam followed Ellie to her place, the bags from the Pic-N-Save on the passenger seat. Before going to the hospital, he'd stopped at the local supermarket for in-gredients. He wasn't much of a cook but he could do a simple stir-fry and rice. Glancing at the white bakery box with its bright blue lettering on the passenger-side floor, he grinned.

He pulled in behind Ellie's car and cut the engine. Scooping up the box, he stuck it in one of the bags and got out. His chest tightened as he followed her up the stairs. Being back in Loon Lake with her felt comfort-ing, secure. But that was crazy. Why would he need comforting?

Following her into her kitchen, he set the bags on the counter. "Before I forget, someone named Lorena at the Pic-N-Save said to say hi."

Ellie laughed. "Did you tell her you were cooking supper for me?"

"She gave me the third degree as she rang up the stuff. I got the feeling if I said I was cooking for some-one else, I was going to be in trouble."

"Small-town life," she said as she took off her jacket. "Let me go change and I'll help."

"Take your time. I got this." He began pulling things out of the bags.

"There's beer in the fridge if you want. Help your-self, I can't drink it," she said, and disappeared down the hallway.

He pulled the rice cooker off the shelf and dumped in

rice and water before plugging it in. Sipping on a long-neck, he began chopping the vegetables. He was slicing the beef when she came back into the kitchen area; when he looked up, his breath hitched in his chest. A strange combination of feelings, a confusing mixture of lust and fierce protectiveness, filled him. He'd experienced both before but never at the same time. This was like a punch to the gut.

"Liam?"

He blinked. "Huh?"

"What can I do?" she asked, frowning when he didn't respond.

"Just stand there and look beautiful." He winced when the casual, teasing tone he was going for fell short.

She sighed and shook her head. "That's hardly productive."

"Then tell me about your day." He poured oil in a pan and adjusted the burner.

She got dishes down and utensils from the drawer, telling him how the EMTs brought in a man having a psychotic episode. "Luckily, Riley and another deputy came in with him."

"Damn." He paused in the middle of adding the vegetables to the pan. He'd heard stories from EMTs about how volatile those situations could get. The thought of Ellie—his Ellie and their babies—caught in the middle of something like that chilled him. "Do you think the ER is the best place for you?"

She set the plates and utensils on the counter with a clatter. "What's that supposed to mean?"

"I know how these situations can go bad. You could've been hurt trying to defuse it." He stirred the vegetables and removed them from the pan once they'd started to soften.

She put her hand over her stomach. "These babies are very well protected at the moment."

"I wasn't talking about them. I was talking about you. You, Ellie, *you*." He pointed at her to emphasize his point, adding the thinly sliced meat to the pan to brown.

"I'm an adult. I don't need someone hovering."

"Since when is being concerned about your safety hovering?" He recalled the time Meg told him how Ellie had gotten beaned by a foul ball during a game to raise money for new water and ice rescue equipment for the EMTs. He took a sip of his beer and put the vegetables back in the pan with the meat. "And should you be playing softball?"

"Softball? It's October. What are you on about it?" She planted her hands on her hips and glared at him. "Oh, wait, I get it. We wouldn't even be having this conversation if I wasn't pregnant, would we?"

The rice cooker clicked from Cook to Warm. He shook his head. "I can't answer that because you are pregnant."

"I assure you, pregnant or not, I can and do take care of myself. I don't need you—"

He turned the burner off and put the meat and vegetables on a platter. "Your supper is ready. We should eat before it gets cold."

She opened her mouth and closed it again. He set the hot pan in the sink where it sizzled when the faucet dripped. With a strangled sound she went to him and put her arms around his waist, pressing her front to his back.

He grabbed her hands in his and turned around, putting her hands back at his waist, and held them there.

She looked up at him. "Why are we arguing?"

He shook his head. "I'm sorry if I worry about you. And I mean *you*. I'm not saying I'm not concerned over the babies, but it's you I think about, Ellie."

"That's good because I think about you, too, Liam." She gave him a squeeze. "And I appreciate you making me a healthy supper."

"Better than a peanut-butter sandwich?"

"Much."

"You haven't tried it yet." He wasn't much of a cook, but stir-fry was pretty easy and healthy.

After eating seated side by side at the breakfast bar, Ellie insisted on cleaning up while he found them something to watch on TV. He decided not to argue with her. Since he didn't do much of the cooking at the firehouse, the guys usually put him on cleanup.

Taking a seat on the couch, he picked up Ellie's pregnancy book from the cushion next to him. He opened the book to the place she had bookmarked.

"Ellie?" His voice sounded strained to his own ears.

She had a bookmark on the chapter about engaging in sex during the different stages of pregnancy. Well, well, well. So, did Ellie have this on her mind? Or was she simply reading the book cover to cover and happened to stop there?

"Ellie?"

"Hold your horses. I'm coming." She came into the living area carrying the bakery box and napkins. Her gaze went to the book in his hand and she stopped short, eyes wide, cheeks pink.

He held up the book. "Interesting reading."

She put the box of cannoli on the coffee table and sat down next to him on the sofa. "I'll take that."

"But I'm not done reading this fascinating chapter yet," he said, and winked.

She tried to pry the book out of his hands, but he was holding on tight.

"I think it's important we read this together. You know, share *all* aspects."

"That's because you're reading the chapter about sex."

"We could read it together," he offered.

She narrowed her eyes. "Just this one? Or all of it?"

"I guess if I was there for the good stuff, I should be there for the…uh, other stuff. Huh?" Leaving Ellie alone to handle all of this would be unforgivable and he liked to think he was better than that.

"Well…" She canted her head to one side as she studied him. "We could start with this particular chapter and then move on to some of the others."

He tossed the book onto the coffee table and jumped up.

She lifted an eyebrow. "No book? Does this mean you're going to wing it?"

His gaze bounced between her and the book. "Is there something special I should know?"

"Not really. I'm not that far along."

That was all he needed to know, as he placed his arm behind her knees and swept her high up into his arms.

"Liam! You're going to hurt yourself."

He grunted and staggered but kept her close in a firm grip. "Now that you mention it…"

"Hey, I haven't gained that much weight, especially with all the nausea."

"If you say so," he teased. He was enjoying the way her eyes sparkled.

"Brat. Put me down," she said, then looped her arms around his neck.

He shook his head as he headed toward the bedroom. "Momentum is on my side."

"Why are you even doing this?" She tightened her hold on him.

"What? You saying you aren't impressed?"

"Maybe if you weren't grunting so much."

He stepped into the bedroom and set her down gently. Straightening up, he put his hands on his back and made an exaggerated groaning sound.

She studied him with a sly smile. "I guess this means you won't be able to—"

He put his hands around her waist to fit her snugly against him. "Does that seem like I'm incapacitated in any way?"

She put her arms around him and nuzzled his neck. "Hmm… I might need further convincing." She kissed him. "Just to be sure."

"Mmm." He nibbled on her earlobe. "Should we get some of these clothes off?"

"Sounds like a plan," she said and pulled her sweatshirt over her head.

His gaze went to the small swell of her stomach. His babies were in there. Without conscious thought, he dropped to his knees and pressed his cheek against the taut skin.

Her hands were in his hair, her nails grazing his scalp as he put his arms around her. The moment might have started as sexy teasing but this was suddenly something more. He searched for words, but the tangle of emotions inside him prevented them from forming.

Her fingers tightened in his hair. "Liam?"

He might not have the words but he could show her what she meant to him.

Rising, he took her hand and led her to the bed, where he quickly disposed of the rest of her clothing.

He caressed her breasts and the areas around her nipples. "Have these gotten darker?"

"Yeah, it's increased pigmentation from…" She swallowed audibly. "Sorry, TMI?"

"You know I'm a sucker for nurse speak." He grinned, then sobered. "You're beautiful, Ellie."

She looked up at him. "And you have too many clothes on."

He reached around her and pulled the covers back. "Get in and I'll take care of that."

He left his clothes in a pile and slipped into bed, taking her into his arms.

Unlike the first time, when they'd both been so eager, he took this slow to demonstrate how much she meant to him. Even if he hadn't said the words.

Afterward, Liam settled her against him and rested his cheek against her silky hair. They worked as a couple and he dared to think about their future. Together.

Chapter Fifteen

Ellie stepped out of the shower the next morning still glowing from the previous night's lovemaking. Dared she hope they had a future together? She smiled to herself as she grabbed a towel from the rack. He might not have come out with the words she longed to hear, but then neither had she.

Liam was taking her to Aunt Polly's, a local restaurant known for its pancakes. Maybe after that she'd—

All thoughts scattered as she felt a slight swelling under her left arm. She shook her head and swallowed back nausea. A swelling where the axillary lymph node was located wasn't good.

Of course there could be any number of non-lethal explanations but her mind insisted on taunting her with cancer. Fighting the urge to curl up in the fetal position on the floor, she wrapped herself in her ER nurse persona and called to Liam.

He popped his head in the doorway and his eyes widened and a grin spread across his face. His smile was her undoing and she choked back a sob.

"Ellie, my God, what is it? What's wrong?" He stepped inside her small bathroom.

"It's here." She lifted her left arm.

"What? What's there?" He stood in front of her.

"A lump…the axillary lymph node is enlarged," she whispered.

His gaze met hers. "Are you sure?"

"Of course I'm sure," she snapped.

He pulled her into his arms. "I only meant that we shouldn't panic. Maybe you bumped yourself."

"Don't you think I've been through all those excuses already? I think I would have remembered bumping myself under my arm. It's not sore or black and blue like a bruise." She buried her head in his chest while he rubbed her back.

They stood locked in the embrace, the only sound was that of a sports show coming from the television in the other room.

Sighing, she pulled away. "I'll need to get a biopsy."

Liam sucked in his breath. "Okay. Where and when do we get one?"

If only it was that easy… Well, it was, but those were the mechanics. The emotions that went along with it weren't. Especially now with her pregnancy. And Liam. Whatever they had was just beginning. She shook her head. Maybe her parents were right not to want— No! She refused to give in to defeatism. "You make it sound like ordering something off the internet."

His fingers were shaking when he reached out. Using

his thumbs, he wiped the moisture from her cheeks. "I'm sorry. I only meant—"

"No, I'm sorry. I shouldn't take my anger out on you." She sighed. "Let me get dressed and I'll make some calls."

Sometimes being an ER nurse, not to mention a resident of a small town like Loon Lake, paid off. Ellie was able to get a biopsy scheduled for that afternoon with her oncologist.

Liam insisted on taking her to breakfast as planned, telling her sitting around and brooding wasn't doing either one of them any good. She appreciated his attempts at proceeding as normal. At the same time they annoyed her. But she had to eat for the sake of the babies so she agreed.

After the restaurant, Liam drove them to the doctor's office. He was by her side and yet…

She clung to his hand in the waiting room, but thoughts of her parents clamored in her mind. Was this how it started for them?

The oncologist, a kindly man in his fifties, carefully examined a cut on her forearm. "This could be our culprit."

"But it doesn't appear to be infected," Ellie told him.

"And maybe your immune system is doing its job and fighting it off." The doctor pushed his glasses on top of his head as he looked at her. "We'll do some tests just to be certain, but I don't want you to worry. We'll have the official results early next week."

Back at home, Ellie tried to take the doctor's advice and remain optimistic. She pretended to read her textbook while Liam fixed her toilet that kept running.

She'd told him she'd put in a work order with the management company but he'd insisted. Not that she could blame him. Doing busywork was probably his coping strategy.

She heard him on his phone and soon he came out of the bedroom with his duffel bag: the one he used when going back and forth to Boston.

"What's going on?"

He looked up from his phone, a flush rising in his face. "I was asked to take an extra shift."

She'd heard him on the phone, though she hadn't heard it ring. Had he called looking for an excuse to escape? She immediately felt guilty for even thinking he'd do something like that.

He ran his hand through his hair, a muscle ticking in his cheek. "It's my job. Something I will need to support these babies."

"Are you sure you're not taking it to escape?" She hadn't meant to challenge him like that, but it hurt that he'd chosen work over her.

"Escape?" He scowled at her. "What the heck does that mean?"

She scuffed the toe of her sneaker on the rug. "Maybe it means that going to work is preferable to being trapped here with Cancer Girl?"

"Why would you even say something like that?"

"You see how my parents are. My dad used work to escape and look what it did to them."

"We're not your parents."

No, her parents were in a committed relationship.

When she didn't respond, he made an impatient motion with his hand. "The doctor said you won't have test results for three days at least. I'll be back once the shift is done. You make it sound like I'm deserting you."

You are! She swallowed and tried to remain calm but it was getting harder. Was this how her mom felt when her dad buried himself in work? Like he deserted her when she needed him? She resisted the urge to act childish by stamping her feet or using emotional blackmail by crying and carrying on. "You're absolutely right, Liam, but I also can't help feeling abandoned. I'm sorry and it might not be fair, but that's how I'm feeling right now. You didn't even consult me."

"I didn't realize I had to." He rubbed the back of his neck. "I'm going to work, not out partying, for crying out loud."

"I know it's irrational but feelings just are…they don't always subscribe to what's rational." It hurt to have him point out that they didn't even have enough of a relationship that he would consult her.

He heaved a deep sigh. "We're in this together."

She glanced at his duffel sitting by the door. "If you say so."

His gaze followed hers and he frowned.

"Could you have refused?"

"It's my job." He shook his head, his face a blank mask.

"My father had a job, too. I saw what my cancer did to my parents, to their relationship. For a while I blamed myself. I was convinced it was all my fault but now I know better. Cancer happened *to* me. I'm not my disease. And I'm sorry if you can't handle it, but that's not my fault."

"I'm not deserting you, Ellie," he said, and shook his head. "I need a little time and space to process all this."

"And that's fine. I understand that." She stuck out her

chin. "I can give you time and space, but I refuse to be in a relationship with a ghost."

Three hours later, Liam walked into the station with Ellie's words echoing in his head. Leaving Ellie alone while she waited for the biopsy results was a cowardly move. But the emotions he'd been trying to deny had threatened to overcome him, so he'd run. He wouldn't blame Ellie if she hated him. He hated himself. By rules, the department couldn't force him to come back early but he hadn't said no. He hadn't said no because he'd panicked. From the moment he'd walked in on Ellie in the bathroom, he'd been unable to take a deep breath. His insides were a tangled black mass threatening to choke him. It was his ma, and to a lesser degree his friend and mentor Sean, all over again. He was going to lose Ellie and it was going to hurt more than the other two combined.

He went about his duties at the house by rote, his mind refusing to be calmed by the familiar routines.

Had he honestly believed being away from Ellie would make his black mass of emotions hurt less, make the panic disappear? Instead, being away increased the pain a thousand times over. He called to check in and they engaged in what could only be described as a stilted conversation.

Had he made the biggest mistake of his life by leaving?

He shook his head and threw the chamois cloth over his shoulder and stood back to check the shine on the engine he'd been polishing instead of watching a movie with the other guys.

"Chief wants to see you, McBride."

Liam nodded and tossed the chamois to the probie. "Have at it, Gilman."

What could the chief want? He hovered in the doorway to the office. "You wanted to see me?"

Al Harris stood up and held out his hand across the desk. "Let me be the first to congratulate you, Captain McBride."

It took a minute for the words to penetrate. Captain? Him? He'd done it. He made captain at a younger age than his dad.

He shook Chief Harris's hand and tried to feel something other than numb.

"You don't look like someone who has just accomplished a lifelong goal."

Yeah, why didn't he feel more? Sure, he was proud, but even that was fleeting.

"Okay, now, sit your ass down, McBride, and tell me what the hell is wrong."

The next morning, after his shift, Liam went straight to the white, Cape Cod–style home where he'd grown up and his dad still lived with Doris. He always had mixed feelings returning here. In the beginning, it was comforting because he felt his ma's presence. But that had faded and this was now as much Doris's home as it had been Bridget McBride's.

He rang the bell and waited. The rhododendrons his ma had loved so much needed trimming, but it was too late in the season to do it now. She had taught him they needed pruning immediately after they finished blossoming or you'd be cutting off next year's flower buds. Helping her trim them one day had actually been punishment for a transgression he no longer remembered.

He rubbed his chest, recalling how, that same day, she'd bought him a treat from the ice-cream truck and let him eat it before supper. She'd winked and laughed as they sat on the front steps eating their ice cream.

Doris answered the door, surprise and pleasure evident in her expression. "Liam, it's good to see you. C'mon in."

"Hi, Doris, is my dad here?" He gave Doris a quick hug and she kissed his cheek.

"Yeah, he's out back if you want to go on through the house." She stepped aside. "Can I get you anything? We've already had breakfast but I can get you coffee or a muffin."

"I'm good. Thanks. I can't stay long."

"How's Ellie doing?" Doris asked as they went through the kitchen to the back deck.

"She's doing good." Other than a cancer scare and being left to face it alone, but he wasn't about to get into all that right now. "She's looking forward to the second trimester which is supposedly much easier."

"Normally, yes, it is but I've never been pregnant with twins."

"That makes two of us."

She laughed and opened the door. "Tim? Liam's here to see you."

His dad paused in the middle of raking leaves and waved. Liam went across the deck and down the steps.

"So glad you're here. I wanted to congratulate you myself, Captain." His dad stuck out his hand and pulled him in for an awkward shoulder hug.

"You knew?" Liam asked when they pulled apart.

"I may have heard something." Mac said and grinned.

"I haven't been gone from the department for that long. I still know a few people."

"Thanks." Liam cleared his throat.

Mac frowned. "What's wrong? You don't look like a man who has just gotten what he's been working toward for years."

Liam swallowed. How was he supposed to explain how hollow he felt? Sure, he was proud of making captain but after running out on Ellie the way he had, all he could think about was how much he'd hurt her. *Selfish much, McBride?* Why was he thinking about his own pain? He should be there comforting Ellie, helping her deal with her pain. Had he thought that, if he wasn't there, he'd be able to better handle the fear?

"What's on your mind, son?" His dad leaned against the rake.

Liam explained what had happened. He hated admitting his cowardice but he couldn't hide from it any longer. "Ellie found a lump and I shut down. I'm not sure I have the kind of courage you had to open myself again to love someone I might lose."

"It's not courage." Mac shook his head.

"Then what is it?"

"It's finding something that's more important to you than your fear." Mac met Liam's gaze. "Is Ellie that important thing for you, son?"

Ellie retrieved her jacket and closed her locker with a sigh. Liam had barely been gone twenty-four hours and the pain of missing him still throbbed, an ache that wouldn't go away. He'd texted earlier in the day but had been vague when she'd asked if he was coming back today, saying he would try but had some business to take care of first.

Had she pushed him too hard? Demanded too much? She pulled the jacket on and grabbed her purse. Maybe she wanted more than Liam could give. That wasn't his fault, nor was it hers. It was just…sad.

She stretched her neck, trying to muster up some energy as she dug around in her purse for her keys. Trudging out to her car, she glanced up and stopped in her tracks. Liam was leaning against her car, arms crossed, head bowed.

"Liam?" She continued walking toward him.

His head snapped up and he blinked, searching her face. "Hey."

She stopped when she was right in front of him. "Is everything okay?"

He reached out and rested his hands on her shoulders, gently massaging them. "It is now. Have you had any news yet?"

She shook her head, not trusting her voice. The look shining in his eyes was making something inside her spring to life, something that resembled hope. Hope was dangerous. Hope made you do things, say things. Hope could be devastating, even if you were careful.

He squeezed her shoulders. "We need to talk."

Talk. Yeah, they needed to talk, but for the moment she was relieved to see him. She did her best to tamp down the hope clamoring for freedom. He might want to talk about logistics or shared custody once the babies were born.

He was peering at her expectantly. Right. She hadn't answered him. "Okay. Come back to my place?"

"I have something I want to show you first, if that's okay."

She nodded, still trying to figure out his mood.

He took her hand in his. "Let's take my truck. We can come back for your car."

"W-what did you want to show me?"

"Our future," he said as he opened the passenger door.

Her mouth dropped open and she stared at him. He put his thumb under her chin and closed her mouth before giving her a chaste kiss.

"Liam, what in the world is this all about?" She still couldn't figure out his mood. He seemed a combination of excited and apprehensive. Or maybe she was crazy. Pregnancy hormones—times two!—were making her giddy.

"I need your opinion on something." He slipped behind the wheel but turned toward her instead of starting the engine. "I need to apologize for taking off on you. I shouldn't have done that."

"And I shouldn't have accused you of abandoning me." She sucked in a breath. "I may have overreacted."

He took her hand and brought it to his lips. "I should have explained myself better. I regret how I handled things with my mom, and yet I was doing the same thing with you."

"I know of a good support group for grieving families, if you're interested." She squeezed his hand. "Maybe we could both benefit from it, but first, I have to see what you want to show me."

He dropped her hand and started the truck. Although he didn't say anything else, he glanced at her several times as he drove across town. Clearing his throat, he made the turn into the Coopers' long driveway.

"Why are you taking me to your sister's house?"

"Meg's isn't the only house here." Liam pulled his truck up to the cottage-style home across the yard from his sister's house. Putting his truck in Park, he shut off the engine. Jumping out of the pickup, he hustled around to her side.

"Careful," he said as he helped her out. "This would have been better in the daylight but I couldn't wait until tomorrow."

She stared up at him, puzzled. "I don't understand what we're doing here."

He ran his finger under the collar of his jacket. "Like I said… I was picturing our future."

Her heart stuttered, then pounded so hard she was surprised it didn't jump out of her chest. She glanced down, expecting to see it flopping like a fish on the ground.

He made a sweeping motion with his hand to encompass the large, open yard between this house and his sister's. "I see kids—our kids and their cousins—running around this yard. Maybe even a dog of our own chasing after them. Baseball games, touch football, along with some hot dogs and burgers on the grill in the summer."

He turned so he was standing in front of her and took both her hands in his and cleared his throat. "I love you, Ellie Harding. No matter what. Now and forever. In sickness and in health. Will you marry me and live here with me?"

Her mouth opened and closed like that fish she'd been imagining a few moments ago. "But…but what about your job? Your house in Boston?"

"When Chief Harris called me in to tell me I'd made captain, we—"

"Wait…what?" She took her hand out of his and jabbed him in the shoulder. "You made captain and are just now telling me?"

He shrugged. "It wasn't important."

"How can you say that? Of course that's important."

"Not as important to me as you and our babies. This right here, with you, is what I want. Chief Harris is always asking me when I was going to sell him my three-decker and yesterday I told him to make me an offer. I tracked down the owner of this one and he's willing to sell. So whaddaya say, should we make an offer on this place?"

Overcome with emotion that her dreams were coming true, all she could do was shake her head and choke back a sob. All the color drained from Liam's face and she realized he'd misunderstood. She threw herself at him and began blubbering incoherently.

He held her and rubbed her back. Finally she raised her head. "I love you, too," she choked out.

He grinned, his eyes suspiciously shiny. "So, that's a yes?"

She nodded vigorously.

"Wait…" He set her away from him. "I was supposed to do this first."

He reached into his pocket and pulled out a ring. "It was my mother's. My dad gave it to me today. Will you marry me?"

"Yes."

He slipped the ring on her finger and kissed her. She pulled away first.

"I haven't gotten the all clear yet on the biopsy," she warned.

"And I don't have another job yet," He brushed the hair back from her face and dried her damp cheeks. "We'll work out all the details."

"McBride, are you telling me I just accepted a proposal of marriage from someone who is unemployed?"

"You're not going to let a little thing like that stop you, are you?" He frowned, then laughed. "I'm still employed and will have to divide my time for now. While I was waiting for you to get off work, my dad called to let me know the state fire investigator's office here in Vermont was looking for someone."

"Would that kind of work make you happy?"

He pressed his hand against her stomach. "I have all I need right here with you and these guys to make me happy."

"What if I don't get good news from the biopsy?"

"Then we'd deal with it together. I'm not going anywhere. Ellie. You've got the entire McBride clan with you, for whatever comes along."

Epilogue

Six months later

"Hey, bud, you didn't have to make this a competition to see if you could get here before your sister or your cousin," Liam whispered to his newborn son, Sean, who was staring up at him. He turned to the similar bundle cradled close on his other side. "And you, Miss Bridget, you'll be keeping all the boys in line, won't you?"

His newborn daughter twitched in her sleep and Liam leaned down to press a kiss to the top of her head. He glanced up at Ellie, his precious wife, who, despite the mad dash to the hospital several weeks early, lay smiling at him.

"You done good, Harding," he said, blinking back a sudden burning in the back of his eyes. "Or should I say 'McBride'? You're one of us now, Ellie."

"You didn't do so bad yourself, McBride," she whispered and sniffled, her lips quivering.

He swallowed and his smile faltered as he adjusted his precious bundles in his arms. "I hope both of you heard that, because it might be the last time she says something like that."

Ellie wiggled her feet under the covers. "Meg is going to be so jealous I can finally see my feet."

Liam shook his head and glanced down at his son. "Looks like the women in this family are just as competitive."

"At least now I can put on my own shoes." Ellie yawned and lay back against the covers. "Good thing you and Riley finished the nursery."

Liam nodded in agreement. The last few months had been hectic, what with a wedding, selling one house and buying another, and starting his new job as a state fire investigator. But he wouldn't have traded one minute of it for anything. Even having to wait for Ellie's biopsy results had been worth the nerves. And the celebration when the all clear came back had been—he grinned at the babies in his arms—best kept private.

"What are you grinning about over there?"

He shifted the babies and stood up. "I was thinking how lucky I am and how I can't wait to start this phase of our lives."

She lifted an eyebrow. "This phase?"

Coming to stand next to the bed, he gently lowered their son into Ellie's waiting arms. "Changing diapers, chasing rug rats around the yard, drying tears and retrieving Barbies from toilets."

Ellie yawned again as she cuddled her son. "I guess I better rest up. Sounds like I'm going to be busy."

Liam leaned over and kissed his wife. "I was talking about us. Ellie, we're in this together. For today and always. No matter what the future brings it's you and me together, sharing everything. Partners."

"Intimate partners," she said and laughed.

As always, her laughter drew him close and filled his heart and world with love.

* * * * *

Don't miss the previous volumes in
Carrie Nichols's Small-Town Sweethearts series:
The Sergeant's Unexpected Family
The Marine's Secret Daughter
Available now from Harlequin Special Edition!

#2713 THE MAVERICK'S WEDDING WAGER
Montana Mavericks: Six Brides for Six Brothers
by Joanna Sims
To escape his father's matchmaking schemes, wealthy rancher Knox Crawford announces a whirlwind wedding to local Genevieve Lawrence. But his very real bride turns out to be more than he bargained for—especially when fake marriage leads to real love!

#2714 HOME TO BLUE STALLION RANCH
Men of the West • by Stella Bagwell
Isabelle Townsend is finally living out her dream of raising horses on the ranch she just purchased in Arizona. But when she clashes with Holt Hollister, the sparks that result could have them both making room in their lives for a new dream.

#2715 THE MARINE'S FAMILY MISSION
Camden Family Secrets • by Victoria Pade
Marine Declan Madison was there for some of the worst—and best—moments of Emmy Tate's life. So when he shows up soon after she's taken custody of her nieces, Emmy isn't sure how to feel. But their attraction can't be ignored... Can Declan get things right this time around?

#2716 A MAN YOU CAN TRUST
Gallant Lake Stories • by Jo McNally
After escaping her abusive ex, Cassie Smith is thankful for a job and a safe place to stay at the Gallant Lake Resort. Nick West makes her nervous with his restless energy, but when he starts teaching her self-defense, Cassie begins to see a future that involves roots and community. But can Nick let go of his own difficult past to give Cassie the freedom she needs?

#2717 THIS TIME FOR KEEPS
Wickham Falls Weddings • by Rochelle Alers
Attorney Nicole Campos hasn't spoken to local mechanic Fletcher Austen since their high school friendship went down in flames over a decade ago. But when her car breaks down during her return to Wickham Falls and Fletcher unexpectedly helps her out with a custody situation in court, they find themselves suddenly wondering if this time is for keeps...

#2718 WHEN YOU LEAST EXPECT IT
The Culhanes of Cedar River • by Helen Lacey
Tess Fuller dreamed of being a mother—but never that one memorable night with her ex-husband would lead to a baby! Despite their shared heartbreak, take-charge rancher Mitch Culhane hasn't ever stopped loving Tess. Now he has the perfect solution: marriage, take two. But unless he can prove he's changed, Tess isn't so sure their love story can have a happily-ever-after...

YOU CAN FIND MORE INFORMATION ON UPCOMING HARLEQUIN® TITLES, FREE EXCERPTS AND MORE AT WWW.HARLEQUIN.COM.

HSECNM0819

"Why are you armed with pepper spray? Did something
happen to you?"

She didn't look up.

"Yes. Something happened."

"Here?"

She shook her head, her body trembling so badly
she didn't trust her voice. The only sound was Nick's
wheezing breath. He finally cleared his throat.

"Okay. Something happened." His voice was gravelly
from the pepper spray, but it was calmer than it had been
a few minutes ago. "And you wanted to protect yourself.
That's smart. But you need to do it right. I'll teach you."

Her head snapped up. He was doing his best to look at her, even though his left eye was still closed.

"What are you talking about?"

"I'll teach you self-defense, Cassie. The kind that actually works."

"Are you talking karate or something? I thought the pepper spray…"

"It's a tool, but you need more than that. If some guy's amped up on drugs, he'll just be temporarily blinded and really ticked off." He picked up the pepper spray canister from the grass at her side. "This stuff will spray up to ten feet away. You never should have let me get so close before using it."

"I didn't know that."

"Exactly." He grimaced and swore again. "I need to get home and dunk my face in a bowl full of ice water." He stood and reached a hand down to help her up. She hesitated, then took it.

Don't miss
A Man You Can Trust *by Jo McNally,*
available September 2019 wherever
Harlequin® Special Edition books and ebooks are sold.

www.Harlequin.com

Looking for more satisfying love stories
with community and family at their core?

Check out **Harlequin® Special Edition**
and **Love Inspired®** books!

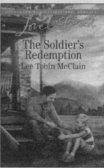

New books available every month!

Meg tensed from head to toe, sucking in her breath as she saw two masculine hands close over the shutters' edges on either side of her body. Then instinctively turned her head to take in light hair, a strong stubbled jaw and blue eyes—no more than an inch from hers.

"I... I..." He smelled good. Not sweaty at all, the way she surely did. The firm muscles in his arms bracketed her shoulders.

"I think I got it if you just wanna kinda duck down under my arm." Despite the awkward situation and the weight of the shutter, the suggestion came out sounding entirely good-natured.

And okay, yes, separating their bodies was an excellent idea. Because she wasn't accustomed to being pressed up against any other guy besides Zack, for any reason, not even practical ones. And a stranger to boot. Who on earth was this guy, and how had he just magically materialized in her yard?

The ducking-under-his-arm part kept her feeling just as awkward as the rest of the contact until it was accomplished. And when she finally freed herself, her rescuer calmly, competently lowered the loose shutter to the ground, leaning it against the house with an easy "There we go."

He wore a snug black T-shirt that showed his well-muscled torso—though she already knew about that part from having felt it against her back. Just below the sleeve she caught sight of a tattoo—some sort of swirling design inked on his left biceps. His sandy hair could have used a trim, and something about him gave off an air of modern-day James Dean.

"Um… I…" Wow. He'd really taken her aback. Normally she could converse with people she didn't know—she did it all summer every year at the inn. But then, this had been no customary meeting. Even now that she stood a few feet away, she still felt the heat of his body cocooning her as it had a moment ago.

That was when he shifted his gaze from the shutter to her face, flashing a disarming grin.

That was when she took in the crystalline quality of his eyes, shining on her like a couple of blue marbles, or maybe it was more the perfect clear blue of faraway seas.

That was when she realized…he was younger than her, notably so. But hotter than the day was long. And so she gave up trying to speak entirely and settled on just letting a quiet sigh echo out, hoping her unbidden reactions to him didn't show.

Need to know what happens next?
Find out when you order your copy of
The One Who Stays *by Toni Blake,*
available August 2019 wherever you buy your books!

www.Harlequin.com

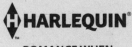